Judy Prescott was born and raised in the busy city of Bristol, the eldest of five children and a daughter to a gentleman's barber shop father and a mother who worked part-time, working around the family commitments.

Moving to South Wales with her husband and two young children over thirty years ago, her grandmother's territory, she hasn't looked back. Writing has occupied her time since ill health halted being able to work a full-time job. Judy, now a widow and a grandmother to six grandsons, continues to write about life in her novels.

To Peter,

We had forty-five years together and wished for so many more. We didn't manage to grow old gracefully, but thank you for all the memories we created along the way.

Judy Prescott

A TIME TO REMEMBER

AUSTIN MACAULEY PUBLISHERS™

LONDON • CAMBRIDGE • NEW YORK • SHARJAH

A CIP catalogue record for this title is available from the British Library.

ISBN 9781398446519 (Paperback)
ISBN 9781398446526 (ePub e-book)

www.austinmacauley.co.uk

First Published 2024
Austin Macauley Publishers Ltd®
1 Canada Square
Canary Wharf
London
E14 5AA

My thanks go to my sister and sister-in-law for reading my novels as I finished them. *A Time to Remember* is a poignant recollection of memories so important to me now and in the future.

Chapter One

'I so hate feet,' said Melinda to the podiatrist. 'They're my worst feature by far.'

Amanda, the podiatrist, continued to tend to her feet whilst she spoke about them. In all fairness, her client's walking aids weren't that bad, in comparison to others she worked with on a regular basis. A few small fungus infected nails had been treated over the previous months and now looked similar to Melinda's other toe nails. Her job today had included filing them down and removing the hard skin from the soles of Melinda's size four feet.

Melinda had been Amanda's friend since moving from England to Wales, they'd known each other for over thirty years now. They lived similar lives, hardworking busy people with family members to help along the way. A friendly disagreement over politics and the like would always end in different conclusions as to how things should be dealt with, whether right or wrong!

On everything else though, they were true companions and always there for each other.

Melinda had needed Amanda's support now, more than ever, and her friend never disappointed her. An ear to listen, a comforting word or two, and a regular coffee time break in one or the other's houses, when time allowed. Not forgetting a bingo buddy, an excuse for a night out.

Today, it was Melinda's unsightly feet that was being given a birthday treat, albeit it being Amanda's profession anyway. She was enjoying it, being pampered for a change. It had felt good and she smiled to herself for the first time in a long, long while.

Melinda's ever ageing facial features had been kind to her. Obvious wrinkles under her eyes and across her forehead would always be there to define her later years, but strangers had never guessed her age to be anywhere close to her actual birth date. Her long dark brown hair required the occasional home dye to cover the recurring grey strands appearing throughout her thick mane.

Melinda's parents' natural colour had remained with them until their older years, perhaps, she'd inherited it from them.

The short stature had been a definite throwback from the family. Just five foot and one inch in height, her siblings had followed her, well, all except one sister that was. The youngest sister stood a good head above the others, intellectually as well as being taller.

Looking down at her feet, Melinda recalled the years they'd been through with a humorous smile on her lips. No wonder they were so ugly!

'What's tickled you?' Amanda asked.

'My life! That's why my feet are the state they are in,' Melinda responded with a grin on her face. She was laughing at her own imperfections.

Amanda's laugh was infectious and Melinda had continued laughing, joining in. 'You're something else, you know that.' Amanda had replied once the laughing had subsided.

Sixty-three years of use her feet had managed, Melinda recalled the four and five inch stiletto heels she used to wear regularly. At work, walking to the shops, everywhere except in the house, Melinda had stood tall in her shoes. A few extra inches to her height had always felt good (and she balanced on them well), accentuated her slender figure and made her feel similar to others, a normal stature. Tich, she'd been called at school, for obvious reasons. The extra inches had added confidence to her wellbeing.

Not any more though, Melinda couldn't wear heels. With arthritic knees for a long time, the wardrobe hadn't included shoes with height for years. A sore point, as she'd loved wearing them. Shoes had always added elegance to an outfit, theoretically, well that hadn't happened for decades now, such a shame.

'Ouch, that hurt! What are you doing to me?'

'Removing the hard skin as you requested. You've suffered worse in your life,' Amanda replied with a tinge of sarcasm.

'Don't I know it. Take no notice of me, Amanda. I should be used to the pain now.' Melinda's mind recalled the years; the recollections of the past. So much had occurred in her life; so, so much.

Melinda was only fifteen years old when she had met Peter, her late husband. A jack-the-lad of his time, hanging out with a gang of mates at weekends, drinking away all of his hard earned weekly earnings. He would finish his Saturday evenings off with a visit to the local fish and chip shop, worse for wear after a few hours occupied in the several public houses nearby. One o'clock Sunday morning, Melinda would serve him Clarks' pie and chips and other choices of food remaining to his mates.

He could hardly stand up at times, his legs threatening to give way beneath him. Whether he had actually wanted food at that time of the morning was debatable, but years later, he had admitted that the visit to the chip shop establishment had been merely to see Melinda. Way back then, Peter had taken a shine to her.

Melinda, a quiet and serious teenager at the time, wasn't remotely interested and it was more than obvious that Peter's showing off was for her benefit alone. Her colleague and workmate, Terry, had registered his interest in her and laughed every time he had walked in. It had been the highlight of their evening, well, sort of!

The slimly built nineteen-year-old, usually dressed in his light grey weekend suit and winklepicker shoes, the fashion of the day then. His shirt buttons opened enough to show a fair amount of chest, and a large silver cross dangling around his neck, wasn't repulsive at all. He looked good as far as male ratings went, but it was his over the top mannerisms that had put Melinda off him. The showing off in front of his companions, the drunken strides across the waiting area of the chip shop; the loud voice, often stuttering his words through too much liquid refreshment. Melinda laughed at his actions, and had voiced her concerns to Terry every Sunday morning, light-heartedly. It had been a regular occurrence that secretly she'd looked forward to.

Less than two years later, Melinda had left the chip shop as an employee, and was now working full-time for a large insurance company. Initially taken on as a filing clerk, she moved up the ladder and was dealing with insurance quotations and policies of various types. Still in contact with Terry, as a true friend, they would often meet up for meals, shopping trips, and ice-skating evenings. He had, on occasions, saved her from disastrous blind dates, and even organised a date with a young lad she was keen on at the time.

Terry would cook for Melinda at his home (his mother's house), regularly treating her like royalty, and made her feel so special. As the eldest of five siblings, she'd felt gratified that someone had wanted to do something solely for her. Buying clothes was his speciality; he was good at helping her decide on an outfit to purchase when Melinda had available funds. Terry's earnings were spent on his somewhat outlandish fashion and looking good was his ultimate goal.

Terry's dress sense, a Gary Glitter copyright with his spiked hair and silver, glittery eyeshadow, his shiny stars dotted around the corner of his eyebrows; his high heeled platform boots, decorated with grey/silver motifs. It had never put Melinda off walking around with him. An honest companion, his looks and appearance had been immaterial, never off putting, and hadn't concerned her in the slightest. A friend, he was, and nothing more.

Between boyfriends, Terry was always there for Melinda. A trip to the cinema to watch a film she'd especially wanted to see, he had willingly escorted her. Ensuring she was home safely, Terry was a true carer. His twin brother, on the other hand, Thomas, was sexual excitement on legs; his persona was electrifying and oh so different from Terry. Thomas's handsome features, his denim jacket and jeans attire, shoulder length straight brown hair; who'd have thought they were twins!

Thomas had never noticed Melinda, even at his mother's house, where he lived with his brother. Their father had passed away when they were young children, babies in fact. There was no attraction there, none whatsoever. Melinda was her brother's friend, that was it. Meet ups for a coffee, with Thomas and his current girlfriend at the time, after an afternoon's shopping spree in town, occurred often. She was Terry's companion, nothing more. At the tender age of seventeen, she had vowed to name any son she might have in the future after the handsome twin brother of her best friend, and years later, had done just that.

Hindsight should have realised Terry's sexual preference, but as a naive teenager, Melinda had never concerned herself on that score. Decades later, Terry was happily married to a similar gentleman, and owned and ran his own hairdressing salon. A true friend, companion, and helper. Terry would always relay fond memories of the past. Inspirational, Melinda had been lucky as a teenager, to have had him by her side. Sadly, his life was cut short several years back, through ill health.

Sam, the lad Melinda had managed to date with Terry's help, had continued their relationship for a good while. She'd been smitten by the neighbour just a few doors away, his parents' running the local delicatessen shop and Melinda's father owning a barber shop at the front of their home and residence. Sam and his older brother had also lived on their parents' shop premises. Melinda continued to see Sam for a few months (a long time then, it had appeared).

A weekly evening out, usually on a Saturday, at the local discotheque. Held in the entertainment room of a small hotel, it had been open to non-residents. Once a week maximum, he'd not afforded to take her out more frequently, but Melinda had never complained. Never a great dancer, a night out with a member of the opposite sex was more a treat than anything else; Sam had a look Melinda had taken a liking to. Not particularly handsome, there was that something that had appealed at the time.

The public house opposite Melinda's residence had admitted her into the establishment of an evening, one of a few places she'd been allowed into. Her mother had worked there as a cleaner for years and the landlord and landlady knew her well enough to behave. Not looking her age, she'd felt honoured to be admitted. Recalling being refused admittance to a cinema due to her looking much younger than her years, Melinda had smiled to herself.

Looking up at Amanda, who had now finished scraping the soles of her feet, she suddenly felt at peace; anger had consoled her head for a while, a long, long while. Her friend smiled too, recognising the old Melinda, but said nothing. Fate, her mother, or something else entirely, had brought her and Peter together, for life; well, his life any roads. At just fifteen years of age, the signs weren't there. Envisaging a relationship with the lad who she'd had no interest in to begin with, none at all, wasn't on the cards. Life had dealt a hand there, something that, over the years she'd been oh so grateful for.

Who would have thought that they would enjoy forty five years together, forty three years actually married? Not Melinda, the obnoxious nineteen year old calling in for Clarks' pie and chips every Sunday morning, the late hours of Saturday evening, that was. Those years gone by, were now a distant memory, a funny and humorous recollection of the past, and now a good one to recall for old times' sake. Melinda smiled again as Amanda wiped her now smooth feet with warm soapy water.

This time, Amanda spoke, softly at first. 'Well, share the memory. What are you thinking about?'

'I was remembering Peter as a person I didn't like very much at the time. I miss him so much, Amanda.' Melinda answered, with a slight tear in her eye.

'We all do.' Amanda responded. 'He will never be forgotten by anyone who knew him.'

'I know, but how did I misjudge him all those years ago? He knew, when I was just fourteen years of age, that he was going to marry me. Dad used to cut his hair in the barber's shop and Peter used to see me taking Dad a cup of coffee in the shop, frequently.' Melinda stopped for breath. 'He knew then, that he wanted to be with me.'

'It all worked out in the end. Don't beat yourself up about it. Well, treatment over for today.'

'How about a meal out tonight, to celebrate?' Amanda asked.

'To celebrate what?' Melinda replied curiously.

'You name the reason. Those smiles, for a start!' Amanda was teasing her now.

'You're on. I will call over to yours after you've finished work.' Melinda paid her friend the going rate for the feet treatment, she always paid the full rate. Amanda knew not to argue on that score. Heading for the door, she waved as she closed the door behind her.

Chapter Two

Melinda scanned her wardrobe that evening for a suitable top to wear with her usual black trousers. Dressing up for the occasion never held the excitement of years ago. An evening out when Melinda was in her teens had involved very careful consideration, and a lot of thought. An outfit required a complete match, from her head to her feet. Colour co-ordination precision, blue and green should never been seen, ever. Shoes had to match the outfit perfectly.

As Melinda added a floral top to her black trousers, stepped into her black flat dolly shoes, and put on her everyday coat, her mind recalled how important things were in her earlier days as opposed to today. Make-up and jewellery, all matched the colour scheme; blue eyeshadow with a blue outfit and an equally colourful necklace of the same shade around her neck, with earrings to match. Detail had been so important then. Looking nice was a necessity, rather than a chore.

Melinda seldom wore make-up and jewellery nowadays. What was the point? Who did she want to impress? Peter was gone now, it wasn't important any more. Living day to day was sometimes harder than others, and learning to live alone after years being a couple took its toll on her. Merely brushing her hair when getting up in the morning was an effort sometimes.

A night out though, with her friend Amanda, had lifted her spirits and she was actually looking forward to a meal out, regardless of her meagre appetite of late. Her feet treatment earlier and an evening out, it had been a definite start to living again. A reason to leave the house, so to speak.

Melinda walked to Amanda's, a fifteen minute walk away. Where they were going, she'd no idea, but for once in a long while she'd felt hungry. Her stomach was grumbling. Now when did she last eat? Melinda hadn't eaten at all that day, she'd suddenly realised. Eating wasn't compulsory any more, as and when had been enough. Meals for one wasn't that exciting. Cooking for two she'd been used to, well up until Peter couldn't eat by mouth, that was.

With a local public house serving decent food nearby, Melinda and Amanda strolled to the normally quiet establishment during weekdays, ordering choices from the menu. Melinda chose lasagne, chips and garlic bread. Amanda settled for the chicken curry, rice and poppadoms. Gazing at the dessert menu afterwards, a decision to abstain from any more food and partake in a glass of white wine instead, had both nodding in agreement.

Amanda's husband had occupied himself by watching sport on the television, bacon sandwiches and a cup of tea, and an evening to himself. A manual worker, he was happy to totally relax for the evening, probably falling asleep on the sofa before Amanda had arrived home. He would have been welcome to join "the girls" for a meal, but was more than happy to leave them talking women's talk over a pub meal without him.

That had also been par for the course with Peter, as the years had passed by. No longer an obnoxious teenager, sleeping before bedtime wasn't out of the question. A film seldom had him seeing the end of it, and a repetition of the film had to be endured again and again, to satisfy his curiosity as to how the finale had evolved. Peter and Amanda's husbands were both very similar in character. Hard working, simple minded beings, content with their lot.

Melinda enjoyed her meal, the company, and the pub surroundings. Not a drinker, two latte's later and plenty of conversation, they headed for their own homes and bedtime. Thanking Amanda for her evening out, Melinda headed towards her humble abode alone, opening the front door onto an air of silence. A silence she so abhorred, but had to get used to. As she headed for the stairs and bed, turning the lights off as she went, another night of broken sleep was looming.

Strange, but the following morning, Melinda got up earlier than usual. The house was tidy, nothing to do inside. Outside was a different matter, but a gardener she wasn't. The sun was shining and there was a gentle breeze blowing. The blue sky looked inviting, so after making herself a cup of tea Melinda sat in the garden and evaluated her life so far. There were so many good times to recall, so outweighing the bad ones.

The sun shone down at her and Melinda smiled to herself. If she'd died tomorrow, she'd no complaints at all, well not many that actually mattered. To others, her life would seem mediocre, but a working class person who had never had any privileges as a child, material wise, wouldn't agree with them. Melinda had been lucky, so, so lucky. To find a soulmate, and share their lives for a long period of time together, was something to be proud of; and Melinda was, so, so proud. Finding Peter at just fifteen years of age and finally agreeing to a date at seventeen had indeed paid off. The chauvinistic attitude in him had been all show, being with his mates had brought out the worst in him. None of his companions were bad people at all. Spending time enjoying a pint, or two, or three, was allowed then and still is today.

Had their first date been eventful? Absolutely. Peter's car was worse for wear and unbeknown to Melinda had no reverse movement working at the time. Driving around the block several times, to park in the petrol station to fill up, had been hilarious. She'd wondered whether she'd done the right thing in agreeing to see Peter at all.

Getting Melinda back home late, a definite no-no with her dad, caused more issues. A polite telephone conversation with Melinda's mum had sorted that out the next day, but neither Peter's nor Melinda's excuse for being late home that night tallied. He hadn't known her parents that well then!

Melinda's sister had answered the door to Peter that first evening. Having a younger sister often mistaken for Melinda caused problems at times. Peter had, too, mistaken her for Melinda. His 'Are you ready?' had taken Melanie by complete surprise.

'Who are you?' was the reply, followed by a loud 'Melinda,' shouted down the hallway.

Melanie grew to love her brother-in-law over the years, as did Melinda's other siblings. Peter was always there to help out when required, one way or another. Sunday afternoons, a leisurely drive indulged, almost always included Melinda's youngest brother and sister. Peter never ever complained, even if he had wanted a few hours as a couple, spending time with just the two of them. Melinda came with four younger siblings and he got used to that, very quickly.

Day trips to coastal areas nearby became frequent during their time dating. A picnic at weekends with Melinda's siblings. No expense spared there! Neither of them earned a lot in their chosen jobs, but a few hours appreciating coastal views rewarded their mundane working week. Peter had been employed in an aluminium foundry, the perks being a roadworthy vehicle costing just the petrol used on a personal level. Tax, insurance and maintenance to the car was paid for by his employer.

Vehicles ranged from Austin A40s, Morris travellers, a bright yellow Ford Cortina, to name just a few. Working for the firm until its closure, there were a lot of different ones in his possession throughout his time there. Peter had worked there from leaving school at fifteen years of age. His boss had paid for his driving lessons and his driving test, all good. Gone was the first car Melinda had been a passenger in, the unforgettable car with the lack of reverse; a vehicle that had actually belonged to Peter rather than the foundry he had worked for. Thank heavens for that!

Had life appeared dull in the earlier days? Not at all. Working throughout the week and spending a few hours of an evening in each other's company, usually in Melinda's family home; there had been no complaints. Weekends were spent together, well most weekends. A journey to somewhere not too far away. Life was much more low key years ago. Expectations were nowhere near as high as they are today.

An evening out in the local public house had occurred often; the public house opposite Melinda's home usually. Melinda had enjoyed her gin and tonic, a brandy and babycham, a cherry B, and the famous Pony (a type of port). Screwing her nose up at the alcoholic choices then, she'd seldom drank anything of the alcoholic variety nowadays, and hadn't for years. As the years had passed, the beverages of olden times were now unnecessary. A cup of tea or a latte coffee sufficed and if honest, were more enjoyed nowadays.

Melinda so missed Peter's company in the house. The kettle constantly boiling for his endless cups of tea throughout the day. Likewise, his drinking habits had changed throughout time. The occasional beer was indeed, occasional. Tea, tea, and more tea was the order of the day. No harm there, though. Proof that, as a couple, they were happy and content in their own unique bubble of life. Affordability aside, neither had required anything more than they actually had, or could afford, until fate had dealt its ugly hand.

Death would inevitably come to each and every one of us. None of us are excluded, it wasn't negotiable. The question was, WHEN? When would it be our turn? Melinda had so looked forward to Peter retiring. Being forced to retire early herself, due to ill health, the plans in her head for the future had held happy thoughts. Sadly, it wasn't to be. The future plans were still there, but unfortunately, Peter wasn't. His death had come early, too early to fulfil their future dreams.

Melinda knew when to stop her thoughts. Negativity wasn't the answer. A walk to the shops was in order to deter her thought process any further. What did she need to purchase? A check through her kitchen cupboards and the fridge established probably two or three items, but the break was required for sanity purposes alone. A distraction, some exercise, and killing time; Melinda's way of getting through each and every day.

Concentration on menial tasks had been almost non-existent since Peter's death. The regular interests of an evening whilst watching the television didn't happen often. Melinda had always been busy doing something else, as well as staring at the box, as a rule. Multitasking was normal for Melinda, par for the course. Now, even the television programmes she usually watched avidly, had no excitement. The ever popular soaps had always been a reason to sit down and relax after nursing Peter.

Take a Break, the magazine issued weekly and monthly, were purchased regularly nowadays. Melinda struggled to complete the crosswords in time to enter their competitions. The deadline date was looming and only half of the crosswords completed. One mad dash to finish them hadn't always worked; her goal unachieved, disappointingly. Reading the stories in the magazine had no timeline and eventually were read, but not immediately.

Melinda had scolded herself for the way she was acting at times. Others were there for her, not always in person, but at the end of the telephone line. Regulars; her sister, her brother (and sister-in-law), and Peter's siblings. His long standing friendship with an old employee, had his colleague ringing and checking up on her periodically. At the age of eighty-five, he was a welcome distraction when Melinda felt out of sorts, so to speak. Friends from afar, almost family, were always there to talk and listen to her, whichever was needed at the time.

With a true friend in Amanda, locally, Melinda had no reason to complain. She was lucky in retrospect. There were others in her position much more isolated and vulnerable, after losing a loved one. Things had required change, she knew that; a wide awakening and maybe some soul searching. Easier said than done, Melinda knew, but well worth the effort on her part.

Familiar faces in the small supermarket had nodded and said hello. Melinda responded in kind. Finding the items on her list and a few extras, she made her purchases. Food fancies on the shelf that hopefully she would eat before the expiry date. Waste was normal at the moment. Lack of appetite and not being bothered to cook for one. Living on her own wasn't all it was made out to be. Melinda had never lived on her own before. Adapting wasn't coming easily.

Good days and bad days, slowly accepting the new way of life. Melinda was determined to cope, but on difficult days had struggled, really struggled. On the whole, though, she'd done well. That was what she'd told herself. Convincing her body that, though, was hard work. How did others in her position cope so well, or like Melinda herself, were they hiding their true innermost feelings? Sadness, anger at being left alone, a little lonely at times. Maybe they were doing just that, with a smile on their face.

Cheese on toast it was that evening, not being bothered to cook anything else more substantial. A cup of tea with and after her meal. Washing up the small amount of dishes and a walk to her friend's house for a few hours. She'd needed company for a while before trying to sleep; trying being the ultimate word. That was yet another story!

Chapter Three

Peter's marriage proposal, just three weeks after their first date, was anything but romantic. An evening out with one of his mates in a local public house, a small back street one at that. Propped up at the bar, Peter had asked Melinda to marry him, in general conversation. Completely out of the blue, very early into their relationship, she'd answered positively, surprising even herself.

There wasn't an engagement ring to hand, a shopping trip to purchase one was required in the near future. Peter's mate had been completely taken aback by his actions, his facial expression had revealed all. Nevertheless, a discussion afterwards, alone, had agreed to announce the engagement on Melinda's eighteenth birthday. Plenty of time to hunt out an engagement ring and arrange a birthday/engagement party in the public house opposite Melinda's home. A combined occasion had made complete sense.

Peter had appeared that certain of who he'd wanted for a wife, Melinda. The earlier comment about knowing he would marry her when she was just fourteen years of age, a mere schoolgirl, had hit home. He was right all along and knew exactly what he'd wanted, unlike Melinda back then. The local fish and chip shop had a lot to answer for, and she had grinned to herself. Hers and Terry's Sunday morning laughs had now become very serious indeed. No-one would have predicted it, not even Melinda.

He had asked her dad for her hand in marriage, after asking Melinda that was, on returning her home that night. Her dad had replied sternly 'Do what you want, just don't ask me to pay for the wedding.'

Clear and to the point was Melinda's dad. No congratulations forthcoming at all. She was young, admittedly, but a positive response would have been nice, whether meant or not. *Okay then*, Melinda thought, she needed a second job to save towards a wedding, whenever that might be. Her full time job could still cover her daily outgoings and pay her lodge to her dad then. She knew how to save and manage her finances, unlike Peter.

Once paid, weekly, the weekend would relieve Peter of his remaining monies after paying his lodge to his dad. Borrowing from his dad to take him through the next week and paying him back every Friday, there hadn't been much left afterwards. Never a saver, was Melinda's husband, ever. They'd have been living in a tent if dealing with finances over the years was down to him, that was for sure. How awful that would have been, and hilarious now!

Melinda had managed to find a second job, two nights a week, in an off licence cum shop, near student accommodation. Peter would pick her up from the insurance company's premises, and deposit her to the off licence, picking her up four hours later. All monies earned there were put by for the wedding day. There had never been any temptation to dip into the funds at all. The engagement/birthday party and Melinda's engagement ring were paid for prior to starting up the wedding fund banking.

Melinda's first encounter with being drunk had happened on that night, the engagement party.

The first of very few occasions in her life to date. Throwing up in his sister's toilet after the party had finished hadn't appeared ladylike at all. Wearing a cream, full length dress, hadn't done her any favours either. What a state it had ended up, well worst for wear. Peter, also completely inebriated through drink, had uttered words not intended. Had the engagement actually happened? Thankfully, things were sorted the next morning, all for the good.

The wedding date was set for a year later in the church not far away, four days before Melinda's nineteenth birthday, due to it being a Saturday. The invitation list was large, due to immediate family; Melinda's dad was the baby of thirteen children and her mum had a brother and a sister. Aunts and Uncles it was for the reception, and parents and siblings. Peter was the youngest of five children, as opposed to Melinda being the eldest of five. The local public house opposite Melinda's home was the venue, and an evening occasion for friends and cousins included afterwards. The wedding was funded completely by Melinda and Peter and had gone according to plan.

Their combined saving over the year leading up to the wedding was compulsive, and they could have afforded a deposit towards a mortgage to purchase a small terraced property. With Peter's mum being ill, a terminal diagnosis, they were asked to reside with them after the wedding. Peter's love for his mum was unfounded, and they'd agreed. Sadly, she had passed away just six weeks later. They had remained with his dad for three years, only moving out when Melinda was pregnant with their son. Needing their own space to bring him up, Peter's dad had understood completely.

'Enough reminiscing,' Melinda had told herself sternly. There were things to be done in the house, nothing urgent, but she could use her time with dealing with some of them. Sat thinking about the past was okay, but time didn't stand still; the hours passed and Melinda needed to busy herself. Memories would always be there to recall, but today wouldn't last forever.

Getting up, Melinda turned the television off in the living room. She hadn't been watching it anyway. The kitchen could do with a tidy up, and she'd fancied cheese and potato pie for food. A mission, it had seemed, but after finding the potatoes in the cupboard, Melinda peeled enough to cook a small dish of her chosen evening meal. With the potatoes on the hob boiling, cheese grated and onion sliced, the kitchen was treated to a thorough clean around.

A smile, afterwards, an achievement at last; she'd not had time to think about anything other than what she was actually doing. With the meal ready to eat, Melinda sat at the kitchen table digesting the food she'd prepared. There was an empty space where Peter should have been sitting, but for once she'd not thought too much about it. Not realising how hungry she'd been, the meal prepared for two days had managed to be eaten in one fail swoop. Success, maybe temporarily, but Melinda was proud of herself. Baby steps, but steps nevertheless.

Amanda had phoned that evening, checking that she was okay. A conversation about nothing in particular, was a welcome distraction to a day spent completely on her own. Melinda had listened to Amanda's day, her regular clients, most of them Melinda had known personally or could at least put a face to. There was no happenings today, nothing much occurred in the village; if it had Melinda wouldn't have been aware of it anyway. Her friend, on the other hand, working in the community, would have been first to have heard any trivial gossip.

Deaths, marriages, babies born; divorces, affairs, not much could be kept secret. Locals had all paid a visit to Melinda on hearing of Peter's passing. Flowers had filled her living room in the first week, but her true friends were still there for her, those who truly cared. She'd been so grateful for that. Sibling telephone conversations were regular, but not being local, visits were infrequent. They had their own lives to live, their own families. Nothing wrong there, life had a habit of not conforming to one's dreams for the future.

Retirement was supposed to have included long, month long holidays to other countries, savouring each other's company at a much slower pace. Drinking in the seasonal sunshine, healthy eating in restaurants overlooking fabulous views. Meeting new friends for the first time, and socialising in whatever vicinity they were in at that particular time. Affordability, the key to everything, but playing at a certain age with the funds they'd had available. All that had been ruined. Melinda was on her own now.

Cancer had a habit of changing everyone's lives, cutting short their dreams for the future, at different ages too. Children and adults, no-one were spared. Upsetting families all over the world, such a horrific disease, freeing only a few but others losing the fight against it. Peter was one of the fatalities, unlike Melinda, who had beat hers. Had Melinda felt guilty? No, but she'd wished she'd gone first at times.

Peter would have argued the case, though. Such a caring person, he would have taken her place throughout her own illness, feeling the pain she had suffered throughout her treatment. He was one in a million, and now he'd gone. Melinda had felt so, so lost.

The soaps were on that evening and Melinda settled herself in front of the television, a cup of tea on the coffee table, along with her mobile phone. Seldom did she hear from anyone of an evening, but sometimes she'd hoped for a familiar voice; an infrequent occasion to correspond with a family member or friend who had a busy life, and little time to relax and make small talk. Melinda hadn't blamed or put pressure on people to contact her, not knowingly anyway. If her mannerisms had shown that, then it truly wasn't meant that way. She had spent over half of her life as a family, her children now grown up with family commitments of their own. With Peter gone, being mollycoddled by them wasn't even an option; Melinda would have hated it.

An independent person usually, being needed was something important to Melinda. Family was everything, and yet, she could on occasions enjoy her own company. Knowing that this was only temporary, and her family were there afterwards, Melinda had always felt safe. Learning to live alone was a lot more difficult than she had anticipated, so much more. Evenings were spent in silence, at times, when Peter was there. Him watching programmes on the television Melinda had no interest in whatsoever, and Melinda on the laptop doing something else completely. The raised noise of action films, and a 'Turn the sound down please,' prompted recognition that both were indeed there together.

With the soaps finished until the future episodes in a few days' time, scanning the television for something else to watch, another cup of tea was required; and getting up from the sofa to stretch her legs. Sitting down for too long sometimes created adverse issues with her health. Melinda struggled to relax completely, nothing knew there though. Par for the course, feeling guilty doing nothing wasn't uncommon at all. Melinda's mind searched for something to do, rather than rewarding herself with some "me" time.

Melinda and Peter had honeymooned in Jersey, just a short plane journey. Neither had flown before, it was a first time for both of them. Weather-wise, the difference wasn't obvious, maybe a few degrees warmer. October it was, and the month was always unpredictable. No rain in sight as yet, all good. St Helier wasn't that big, but there was plenty to explore. The room was standard, nothing to write home about, and above the kitchen. You could smell the food cooking below, and hear some noise at meal times.

The options, as far as culinary delights each evening were concerned, was a difficult one each and every meal time. Being spoilt for choice, Melinda had chosen the fish one night and it was very tasty, she'd thoroughly enjoyed it. Only afterwards did she realise that she had eaten dogfish, something she wouldn't have chosen if she'd known. Just the thought of it!

Getting caught up in the entertainment afterwards, Melinda and Peter had joined in with an adult version of musical statues. Being the last one standing, holding a champagne bucket without the ice, monies had been thrown into the bucket by everyone who had entered. Melinda had won the game and all the cash in the bucket. It was only afterwards that she had realised everyone had known that Peter and her had been newly-weds. Somehow, the game was rigged! No complaints really, but Melinda wasn't one to draw attention to herself, as a rule.

There was a fairground nearby, and both of them had spent a few hours on some of the attractions there, one afternoon. The weather was good, not too cold, and the sun was shining. A browse around the shops, the jewellery shops in particular. A necklace was purchased from the monies accrued the evening before, something neither of them would normally do. They were on their honeymoon, a decent enough excuse.

The week had flown by, Jersey had ticked all the boxes. A pretty escape from Bristol, work and general day to day existence. A first for everything; flying, the Channel Islands, and becoming a pair, husband and wife. They'd had all their lives in front of them and returning to Bristol was just the beginning. Jersey had had a return visit the following year, with Melinda's sister and her working friend and partner. A completely different holiday with the hotel rooms above a nightclub. Noisy on an evening, but otherwise a good time welcomed by all. A lovely break.

They had ventured further afield after that. Holidays became compulsory, even after the children were born. Replacing a hotel abroad for a caravan in Weymouth in the summer, but a well-earned break, nevertheless. All work and no play, as the saying goes. Their children could never complain about not going anywhere, and didn't, even though finances were stretched to afford any break at all.

As the years progressed, a holiday abroad every two years with Peter's family occurred. Some strict saving to raise the funds for the two week sunshine break, but memories will never fade, and there were some fantastic memories to recall, with photographs to prove it. Peter's dad had joined them on a few of the vacations, taken under the families wing after losing his wife. Being pushed around in a wheelchair on one of them, Melinda and Peter's young son had fallen asleep in it. Onlookers cooed and aaarghed, thinking he was disabled. Neither of them had had the heart to relay anything to the contrary.

Melinda smiled, thinking about the earlier years of their marriage. Two young children to love and care for. A wonderful experience that no-one could ever take away. Was life easy? No, but they managed. Good, bad, or indifferent, they were a family united. Both Melinda and Peter had children to fill their time, between work commitments, that was. They got by, and although things were denied due to lack of funds, the children hadn't fared that badly. They were loved. The most important factor of all in life.

Childhood illnesses, bruised knees and legs, on one occasion a nail in their son's head. Don't ask! Life continued busily with no time to sit and wonder about anything at all. All good, Melinda now realised. Peter had wanted three daughters, his dream. Starting with a son, followed by a daughter, then losing baby number three, that hadn't happened. Nevertheless, he doted on his children and would have done anything for them, and did, until his last breath. No question about it, Peter was a family man, first and foremost. His life revolved around doing things for others, never putting himself first. Never idle, never still, his cancer had upset everything he stood for.

Laid on the sofa all day and every day was so out of character for him, but he'd not had the energy to do anything else, at the end. Even listening to music, especially Elvis Presley songs, had upset him. He could no longer sing his idols records due to his voice bordering on almost silent, a whisper would be more accurate. Television programmes held a little more interest, but the majority of the time his head was in the sleeping position, not avidly tuned into whatever was on.

Melinda was lost without him. Coping was hard, so hard. Her days felt like a lifetime, every single one of them. Filling her time alone, was and became, utterly exhausting. The ummph taken out of her body without lifting a finger.

Chapter Four

Getting up the next morning, late as usual, the sun shone through the curtains as she pulled them back. The windows needed a good clean inside; a paid window cleaner sorted out the outside every six weeks or so, thankfully. On a dull, overcast day, it wouldn't have been obvious to see. The dust on the mantelpiece stood out like a sore thumb; the glass coffee table was full of fingerprints, or marks of some sort.

Her day had now appeared to be filled up, cleaning of all things. But Melinda hadn't wanted to, or had any inclination to follow in George Formby's popular single in its heyday "When I'm cleaning windows." Melinda was the only person in the house, and visitors were far and few between. She'd nobody to impress. After a cup of tea and a bowl of cereal, she put her coat on, swapped her slippers for her flat dolly shoes, and walked out of the front door. Her handbag was in the hallway and had been picked up on the way out.

Having her car keys in her free hand, Melinda opened the driver's side of her small car. Where was she going? She'd no idea. All she knew was that staying in the house alone for another solitary twenty-four hours wasn't an option. A breath of fresh air was well and truly needed, and her car was due a drive, having not had any use for several days.

There was enough food in the freezers and her larder to last months. She'd not required any more, and the same could be said for her clothes. Where did she go to wear them now? If Melinda had lost or gained weight since Peter had passed, then that would have been a more than valid excuse to spend money on wearable purchases. She hadn't though, her weight had stayed the same; maybe a few more wrinkles on her face. That hadn't interfered with her body weight, just added years to her age.

Not able to walk that far without pain occurring in her stomach, a result of a twelve hour diep flap reconstruction operation years ago; Melinda's knees had suffered extreme arthritis for years now, as far back as she could remember. Bending down had always been problematic, and not very ladylike at all. Somehow, Melinda had managed most things, even though at times her body had appeared distorted. She had at that moment in time, laughed at herself. Just thinking about some of her awkward positions brought tears to her eyes.

Where could she go? A drive for driving's sake, wasn't Melinda as a rule. She'd needed a reason to venture out in the car, and a more than commendable excuse for spending money; money that couldn't be replenished. Melinda had to be careful with her finances, but when bored would throw caution to the wind and become a little reckless. Nothing too expensive, a bargain hoped for, something to cheer herself up. She couldn't think of anything that was necessary to purchase in the shops she would usually visit, or any item that had taken her fancy previously. Nothing had sprung to mind, nothing at all.

A coffee and cake moment then, her head had indicated. The car had driven itself (almost), veering towards a small cafe in the centre of town. Not that far away, parking in the car park, and paying the fee applicable, the popular cake shop and cafe it was to be. Recollections of Peter and herself frequenting the establishment, after a browse around the shops nearby, caused her to stop and think, initially. A tear attempted to drop, but Melinda calmly walked into the cafe and sat down at a vacant table. Glancing at the menu she realised that this was her future, dining alone, so to speak. Melinda had needed to get used to it, and quickly.

The home-made quiche and salad was as tasty as always, the hot chocolate and cream just as delicious. Looking at the empty seats around her table, and tables around about filled with couples and families, Melinda somehow felt different, left out. One solitary person occupying the table hadn't felt right; not the norm, and so different. Picking her mobile phone up and glancing at it, to kill some time really, she pretended to be busy. Melinda wasn't sure that her new way of life had suited her and questioned her ability to cope, again and again.

As she left the cafe for a browse around the shops, the area of men's toiletries, clothes, and gifts for men were quickly walked past. Melinda had always bought Peter's clothes, shoes being the only time he had physically needed to be there. Her judgement was usually good, both in size and fashion sense. Forty-three years of marriage had perfected what had suited him, nothing too fancy or outlandish. The exception being his Hawaiian shirts, one much brighter and louder than the other. Purchased in Hawaii, whilst on holiday celebrating twenty-five years of marriage, they were two necessary pieces of clothing when karaoke singing on holiday. At least, one of the shirts was always packed into his suitcase. Elvis Presley songs required a Hawaiian shirt!

A small carrier bag full of items were purchased, some necessary, things recalled when seen on display. Other items were bought in the hope that she would fancy a treat on an evening whilst watching the television alone. Savoury snacks always won over sweet fancies, chocolate an occasional preference. If Melinda hadn't eaten them before the grandsons had visited, she wouldn't have stood a chance afterwards. That was the luck of the draw.

Melinda walked slowly back to the car, carrying her goods. Not driving back home immediately, she sat and thought back to Peter's weight loss in the final months of his life. Never ever being anything other than leanly built, he'd looked almost a skeleton when in the bath. It had, on several occasions, reduced Melinda to tears. There was absolutely nothing of him and she had remembered his own mother, shortly before her death, so similar in circumstances, and so soul destroying. Melinda's own mother had only weighed 4 stone 7lbs in her last weeks, but always slim and short, it hadn't appeared quite so dramatic.

How Melinda so wanted the visions of the past to disappear. Focusing on the future was so hard when thoughts of the past wouldn't allow her to move forward. When would the nightmare stop? Grief hadn't a time limit, it could go on for years before living normally resumed. Incorporated in a bubble, trying to escape; Melinda's perception of how she was feeling right now.

Holidays had always helped when day to day routine had required a change. Nothing fancy, a change of scenery, an excuse to relax. Peter would have happily continued working at home or around the neighbourhood instead. Melinda's organising of future breaks, once there, had indeed blown the cobwebs away. She'd known when a break was needed for both of them, and would spend hours on her laptop finding holiday bargains.

Abroad or in the UK, it hadn't mattered. Recalling a two week break in Portugal, Melinda's expression had her beaming at the necessity of her husband's physical appearance being there of an evening. Elvis Presley had sung his heart out to all there, dancing with guests, even singing a duet with some of them. Peter's voice was good, he entertained them with gusto, loving the attention. One evening, after arriving late in the lounge area of the hotel, the applause from everyone there and the "Elvis has returned to the building" had Melinda blushing. Peter had loved it though.

Who would have envisaged a low key hotel with a "pond" for a pool, a three day period of no hot water due to maintenance issues, and apartments requiring complete modernisation, become a holiday never ever to forget. They had occupied an apartment on the twelfth floor, the top one, and Peter would feed a certain seagull daily on the balcony. It had become accustomed to them being there, unusual for a bird of that calibre. Not the type to have a friendly nature at all.

Watching residents walk to and from the adjacent hotel for a warm shower, wrapped in a large towel and another covering their newly washed hair, was laughable. From the top floor, they could see everything around them, and the views were outstanding. Portugal, from then on, was always a favourite on their holiday list, but that particular vacation had become one of the best, for all the wrong reasons!

Elvis Presley, aka Peter, was born when Melinda and her husband had celebrated their silver wedding anniversary in a combined vacation to Las Vegas and Hawaii. A three week holiday and a fabulous journey to areas of the world Peter's idol had visited in his lifetime, short as it was. From the gambling capital of the globe with out of this world hotels; a city that never sleeps and clocks displaying the actual time being far and few between. Food so delicious with ginormous portions where every resident living in the vicinity should definitely have been obese. A city full of glitzy shows and over the top presentation. A once in a lifetime experience never to be missed. Thankfully, they'd managed to visit Las Vegas again, a few years later on, and nothing had changed at all. The experience was equally electrifying and everything sparkled just as before.

Hawaii, in contrast, is an area where gambling is illegal with not one fruit machine in sight. No Wages being their motto, as far as Las Vegas was concerned. Chalk and cheese in comparison, but two beautiful places and both so unique. Peter had felt sorry for the compère of the karaoke entertainment in their hotel of an evening. He had sung his heart out, without one single person willing to pay an American dollar to sing themselves. He appeared to be flogging a dead horse, so Melinda's husband got up from his chair, handed him a one dollar note, and promptly sung Loving You by Elvis Presley.

Peter had looked directly at Melinda whilst singing it, so, so sweet. Her heart had melted and she blushed, hiding her face with her hands to cover it. The compère, whilst listening to him, had approached Melinda, asking whether she had known that her husband could sing so well. She had nodded positively, but usually Peter's nerves had gotten the better of him, and he would watch others rather than try to participate himself.

From then on, Elvis became his karaoke signature on every holiday abroad. Finding a bar to sing in was paramount once they had arrived at their destination, unpacked their suitcases and had drank a cup of English brewed tea, in that precise order. Streets had been walked and walked, to find a suitable evening entertainment venue, before they could totally relax and revel in their holiday. It was all worth it though, the people met on various vacations became firm friends and additions to their ever growing Christmas card list.

Were they both in bed by 10pm every evening? Not a chance! Usually they were still up partying at 4am the next morning. It was what it was, a holiday, a break from day to day regime, and a reason to treat one's self. There wasn't any requirement to find excuses. The time was there to do whatever they had wanted, without judgement, and Peter had loved the karaoke nights and all that it had represented. Age was immaterial, now was important, and making the best of today. Tomorrow wasn't always promised.

Melinda deliberated as to whether she could travel alone, continuing their love of holiday-making. Yes, no, maybe, she couldn't decide. What she could do, was travel with her friend, if Amanda was up for it. Unlike herself, she did have a husband to take into account, so the doubts were highlighted. He had deserved some precious time with his wife, after all said and done.

It was the answer to moving on, whatever Melinda had decided, and required an awful lot of consideration and thought. Courageous she wasn't, but what were the alternatives? Continuing as she was doing wasn't the answer, and Melinda knew it. Her head filled with ideas, some impossible, some were headed perhaps, and others a definite maybe. Suddenly, she had smiled to herself, promptly picking up the laptop and typing in holiday destinations. With pen and paper to hand, a more than possible project in her head, she surfed the web for destinations to suit herself alone, and herself and Amanda. Ideas needed ideas, lightbulb moments, and Melinda had plenty of time to spare in hopefully finding a selection of areas of the world to explore in the future. Repetitions of past countries were more than acceptable, even identical areas of countries visited with Peter.

Melinda scribbled away, made herself a cup of tea, then scribbled away again. As a couple, Peter and Melinda had made future plans to travel to a destination for a whole month, delighting in the sunshine abroad whilst the UK shivered and encountered rainy days after rainy days. It hadn't happened, Peter's illness had stopped it abruptly. Mini breaks in the UK had been taken as best they could between treatment in hospital and long hospital stays.

Just one visit abroad, to Spain for Melinda's sixtieth birthday, had been accomplished. Strict orders from the concerned consultant and three weeks of horrific radiation on his immediate return, but it was something to remember as a family, with highs and lows along the way. A definite vacation fulfilled under difficult circumstances, and thoroughly enjoyed by everyone present at the time. Was it time to venture out again?

Chapter Five

Melinda's daughter had rung that night. A short call wanting her mother to pick her youngest son up from school the next day. Picking him up, usually twice a week, had broken up Melinda's days on her own. Melinda welcomed any excuse to see more of the younger family members. She adored her grandsons and the contact allowed her to see them regularly. The older of the two boys was in the Welsh medium comprehensive school, and a school bus had picked him up and dropped him back home after school lessons were concluded for the day. The bus stop was conveniently placed outside of their home.

The boys' mother was a career woman, constantly pushing herself to higher goals up on the employment ladder. Her husband, as well as having a regular day job, had worked away a lot doing a second chosen vocation. Melinda loved seeing the boys and being involved in their lives. If asked, her own choice of career would have always been family orientated. Not university taught, Melinda was far from stupid, by any means, but priority would always be about her children and the grandchildren.

Likewise, Peter's major concerns were always about people, and he totally idolised the boys; a child rejuvenated whenever they were around. Hiding under the kitchen table when playing hide and seek, throwing snowballs at the boys when the cold fluffy white stuff covered the ground outside in the winter months. He became a child himself, but struggled at the end to compete. His illness couldn't cope with noise. Children always came with loud voices, especially the youngest one. It had appeared impossible to cope with the innocent sounds of fun and frolicking as his cancer diagnosis had neared its conclusion, and ravaged his slim figure.

The willingness to play was there, but the energy had been zapped from his body completely. Moving from his bed downstairs to the sofa at the other end of the living room, was as much as he could manage towards his final weeks on earth. He hated what his illness was doing to him, but refused to give in to it at first, until physically he couldn't comply. Peter's head was giving out positive vibes, but his body signalling a different story altogether. The youngest of the children still spoke about his granddad a lot, and Melinda knew that he would never be forgotten, for all the right reasons. Wanting to find a four leafed clover, granting him a wish, the five year old had wanted to wish his granddad down from heaven. So innocently said, Melinda held her composure, just.

Melinda's daughter was never one to occupy precious time in small talk. Straight to the point, the phone call indicated what was wanted and nothing more. Niceties would never have entered her mind. She'd no time to waste on conversation for conversation's sake. Melinda loved her all the same, for who she was. Proud of her achievements to date, she had more than made up for Melinda's lack of studying.

When all said and done, all Melinda had ever wanted in life was a family, and a job that paid the bills. She'd never hankered after a certain career, or anything more than being able to manage life financially. Her hobby, if she was honest, was exploring countries of the world before her time was up on this planet. She had not done badly so far, and in her head could still go further and continue the escapade she had started with Peter. Travelling alone though, Melinda wasn't used to. Could she actually partake in a journey as a sole traveller? At that moment in time, Melinda was uncertain. A lot more confidence in herself was required, for sure.

Thoughts of Melinda's son entered her mind then. A man now, a handsome one at that (she was biased) with a wife and two boys of his own. Melinda had wished for the child he used to be, the well-mannered, caring and busy boy that he was. Recalling the morning before his birth, Peter had tried to help Melinda. Ringing the GP and relaying his wife's symptoms that morning before heading for work, the GP had convinced them both that Melinda wasn't in labour. Their son wasn't due for another week, as far as dates were concerned.

Advised to take two paracetamol tablets and return to bed, Melinda had laughed. She couldn't even sit down, lying in bed wasn't even an option. Pacing up and down the living room holding her stomach, Melinda had rung her husband, now in work, asking him to return home. The pain was more frightening than unbearable, having never given birth to a child before. At her pace, there would be no tread remaining on the carpet.

Peter had returned home, promptly ringing the local hospital and explaining in detail, his wife's symptoms. 'She's not in labour,' he had added. The GP had told him so.

The nurse, on the other end of the telephone, had asked how he had known that and told him to take Melinda to the hospital as soon as possible. Melinda had already prepared a bag to take to the ward, and picked it up before getting into the car, very awkwardly and still holding her stomach.

On reaching the maternity ward, Melinda had been reprimanded for leaving it so late in getting there. She was indeed well into the final stages of labour. What did the GP know? Their son was born later that evening. A perfect baby, full of dark brown hair, everything in the right place, or so they had thought. Suddenly doctors crowded the cot he was in, causing major concern for both Melinda and Peter, now extremely worried parents. Peter had guessed his weight to the ounce, 6lb 3oz, but something was seriously wrong.

His willy (penis) was abnormal, three holes evident in the tiny part of his body, rather than the usual one. Fountaining into one of the doctor's eye whilst he prodded around, was well worth a naughty giggle and a quiet smile. The problem wasn't life threatening, and could easily be rectified, in time. A small skin tag (a type of wart) hung on one of his tiny ears, something that could also be sorted out with a small skin graph when he had reached a year old. Whether this was genetic, the skin tag, it hadn't appeared obvious at the time. Further down the line though, Melinda's nephew (Melanie's son) and their daughter's youngest son, Peter and Melinda's grandson, were both born with identical skin tags on identical ears.

Quite spooky, just thinking about it. Melinda remembered the television series of years ago, where a horrific facial birthmark had bestowed itself on children of family members with the actual birthmark themselves, an identical scar known as The Mallon Curse. Would the infamous skin tag continue into future generations? Why was it only boys that had inherited it? Melinda pondered a while, deep in thought. A chuckle had erupted from Melinda and she scolded herself for being silly.

His dark brown hair was lost pretty quickly, and by the time he was a year old, replaced with a mop of blond curly locks, falling in uncontrolled ringlets around his face. People often commented; the envy of all the little girls' parents, his hair was his crowning glory. A busy bee, as a toddler, eyes required constant continuous supervision. Climbing out of his cot at just ten months of age, and already walking, Melinda and Peter were seldom allowed time to relax. How their daughter was born, less than three years later, was indeed a miracle. Neither would have lived their lives without them, despite the trials and tribulations of bringing them up; the sleepless nights were uncountable, running up and down the stairs returning their son to bed, yet again and again. Being parents was much harder than they had ever predicted.

Melinda's memory of both her children as babies and beyond would never fade. Born almost five weeks after her due date, Peter and Melinda's daughter's skin was wrinkled and dried up, prune like, confirming that she was indeed well overdue. Recalling passing her own birthday, her mother's, and her youngest sister's before entering the world, Melinda had almost given up on the baby's arrival. She had carried the extra weight well, in the circumstances.

Life from then on was all about family. Visiting Peter's dad every Saturday afternoon with his siblings, a few hours getting together for a Chinese meal from the establishment opposite his house. Melinda's mum was there to help with her grandchildren when needed and visits to her house were frequent. There were times when Melinda and Peter's home had siblings children there for more than a few hours and vice versa. Melinda's youngest sister had five children and Melanie had two. Both of her brothers had one child each. Cousins playing with cousins was what life was all about and how things were meant to be. With the children all grown up now, two of the boys deceased at tender young ages, they all had their own lives to live, and their own individual families to attend to.

Melinda had felt completely lost since Peter had passed away. Frightened of butting into someone's privacy and feeling unwanted, she feared rejection and hadn't wanted to impose on family members too much. She soldiered on relentlessly, trying to cope on her own and be as independent as possible. There were moments when Melinda had felt like a spare part, and had wanted out of the equation, but she could be strong the majority of the time, and she persevered.

Amanda was the glue that forced her to hold on. A friend when required, an ear to listen, and a true companion to spend a few hours with, in and outside of the house. Melinda would get used to her new way of life eventually, her new found freedom to do whatever she had wanted, whenever the fancy had taken her. Unfortunately, Melinda couldn't convince herself on that score, not yet anyway.

Melinda's life had always been about organisation, from a very early age. Lists on paper and in her head, she'd evaluated her day by what was required to be done there and then. The next weeks' to do list was written down somewhere and usually complied in detail, to the letter. When younger, her brain would store the details without any forgetfulness, sadly not today though. A calendar had held important dates for referral. Life was all about organisation and always had been.

The living room in their house, the days before Peter had passed away, had resembled a rubbish tip. Everything was out of place in order to allow him to live out his final hours at home. The hospital bed required plenty of space, and the nurses attending to him needed plenty of vacant room to take care of him. The oxygen floating around the space Peter had occupied, its large tank with pipes attached and draped across several areas of the room, had looked messy. The equipment was necessary, essential to give Melinda's husband the best palliative treatment and end of life care.

If Melinda was honest with herself, the disorganised chaos had played heavy on her mind. She'd hated it, but knew that Peter hadn't wanted to die in hospital. The day he had been told by the junior doctor, alone, he was dreading not being able to return home, and had told Melinda his feelings. Mess or no mess, Peter had got his wish, and had ended his days at home with his family around. She was grateful for that, at least.

Melinda had always wanted to plan the days ahead of her, even if plans hadn't been adhered to completely. If most of the list was done for the day, she was happy enough, adding the chore undone to the next days' list. She had lived by this method for years and it had usually worked fine, except for the odd day or two. Catching up with everything planned wasn't impossible, as a rule. Years had gone by, when she had worked for a living, and life had become busy, busy, busy. Picking up her eldest grandson from her daughter's house and dropping him off at the local crèche, before driving to work and completing a twelve hour shift; followed by a food shop in Tesco before eventually returning home.

She could cope with a twenty-four hour routine then, even if, at the end of the day she was totally exhausted. Looking back now, they were the good old days. No-one was ill, no life or death decisions to make, merely living for the moment and working to pay the bills and saving for a holiday or two. It was nothing that anybody else of the same ages weren't doing. It was called living!

Little bumps now and again had been ironed out without too much complication, and the more difficult decisions sorted themselves out eventually. Those that were unresolved, stayed unresolved, but daily life continued and routines remained unchanged. Anybody who believed that everything was picture perfect all of the time would be lying, and merely putting on a brave face.

Melinda's cancer diagnosis had come when she was fifty-four years old, and a shock to the family. Even more so to Melinda herself, as she'd thought she was going through the menopause. The symptoms were similar, but a routine mammogram had shown something completely different. Peter's mother had passed due to the deadly disease, as well as his eldest sister. Hearing that his wife was suffering too, had Peter in tears. Not something he had wanted to hear.

Trying not to think about things, Melinda continued working until a few days before her first operation. It had stopped her thought process going berserk, and being the day of The Grand National horse race, she'd not had time for much else. The yearly event in the bookmakers was about to become manic, the famous race a must for gamblers and families alike. Melinda had worked the day after the horse race too, but hadn't worked since. Routine and planning had gone out of the window, never to resume to normality ever again.

Chapter Six

Tuesday was usually bingo night for Amanda and Melinda. A gambling establishment that sometimes had them winning houses and increasing the monies in their purse. More often than not they were out of pocket, but looked on it as an evening out, rather than a waste of money. A meal out, a hot beverage and several games of bingo throughout the evening was indeed good for them both.

With Melinda's commitments in picking up her grandson from school, and Amanda's commitment to her work and her family, the weekly socialising was well worth the expense even if they had been unlucky in hitting the jackpot, or securing a share of the link bingo sessions. An excuse to get out of the house was a good enough reason to enter the bingo establishment, not that either of them had needed to answer to anyone else (except maybe Amanda's husband). They were adults, after all. Maybe grown up kids was a better description, at times.

Peter had never minded her weekly few hours away from him. He would happily sit watching his favourite programmes on the television, munching dairy milk chocolate or cake. A tin of Quality Street always contained empty wrapper after empty wrapper and Melinda had to pull them all out before making a choice herself. He was happy, and that was all that mattered. Peter had always had a sweet tooth, since knowing him in her teens. A separate shelf in the larder filled with favourite sweet varieties, was his and the grandsons' first point of contact in the kitchen, whatever the time was.

As Peter's health had declined, the weekly bingo sessions weren't always on cue, but wherever possible they did go ahead. A few hours break from nursing her husband usually did the trick, and allowed a little socialising for the pair of them. How Melinda had missed looking after Peter now. Having so much time on her hands and nothing concrete to do, was depressing. Sure, Melinda could clean things around the house that really hadn't required any action just yet, but she couldn't see the point in it, to be perfectly honest.

Getting up late most mornings was the answer, as Melinda had seen it. What was there to get up for anyway? Late nights and late mornings became a habit, and breakfast had gone out of the window completely. One meal lost each day, the probable reason Melinda had had no interest in eating decent meals, or looking after herself. What would her husband say if he was here now? Melinda knew, without a doubt, that she would have been reprimanded for her actions of late. Peter would have had severe words with her, as Melinda would have done if the roles were reversed.

Melinda's regular voluntary work in the local cinema had been put on hold to care for Peter, whether he was in the hospital or at home. The first eighteen months' of his illness had included regular hotel or caravan breaks, in between the hospital treatments and appointments. The treatments were plentiful, some with severe side effects, but had held the cancer back in the beginning. Mini holiday breaks in the UK had helped both Peter and Melinda cope with everything that was put in front of them. A five day caravan vacation was just what the doctor had ordered, with different scenery to appreciate almost every time.

Fishguard in Pembrokeshire, West Wales, became a favourite area to pursue and explore. Finding like-minded people to converse with in the small clubhouse, had held fond memories every time they had booked the caravan site. With a working class background, cheap and cheerful was usually preferred opposed to dressing up and being waited on. Peter had loved it there and it had done wonders for his well-being. A leisurely cliff walk along the coast, a coffee and cake pit stop before walking back, or a mug of tea, in Peter's case. A custard slice, the bigger the better, would send Melinda's husband into a child-like sense of euphoria. The Fishguard Bay hotel, looking high above the immense and picture perfect sea below, was a place they had both promised to stay in, for a few spoilt days in the future. Melinda had stayed there on their wedding anniversary, alone; Peter was never going to be able to experience the hotel, but Melinda had managed to do it for them both.

The chemotherapy, radiotherapy, and at the end, the immunotherapy, was coped with as best as Peter could. He could still manage a smile and a joke or two, and always remained positive throughout everything thrown at him. The biopsies, blood tests, and consultant's appointments became a regular part of life; they never appeared to phase him, surprising the nurses in charge at almost every meeting. Melinda had been the one on tenterhooks, fearing the worst at the best of times. He would hold her hand to steady it, when the results were actually about his health rather than her own.

Melinda had recalled her own breast cancer diagnosis and telling the consultant at the time to get on with her treatment, before walking out of the hospital with her head held high. Not dissimilar to Peter, the treatment and operations were far from easy. A twelve hour operation to remove one breast and a reconstruction using her stomach fat, was a nightmare for Peter and their daughter, both waiting patiently for her to wake up from the recovery room. There were hurdles in the way of Melinda's treatment, with both breasts becoming infected after the operation. An abscess had required treating for months' afterwards, the hole in her good breast that is now always evident. The foul smell when it had become apparent, is something Melinda and her daughter will never ever forget. She could recall the putrid odour, even now.

The one thing Melinda had going for her, was that her diagnosis wasn't terminal. Medical staff had good reason to believe that she could beat the deadly cancer that was ravaging her body. Losing a part of her body and damaging other parts of it was inevitable, but they were hopeful at destroying the pesky cells not needed in the human body. As of this moment, things still look promising, nine years down the line.

Peter's diagnosis wasn't remotely as clear cut, unfortunately. The prognosis was that the lung cancer was inoperable and terminal, but controllable. For how long though, was not determined. Holding out for more than five years had sounded impossible, in consultants' language. The fact that the cancerous mass was evident in the left lung, near the heart, had rendered it inoperable. Purely bad luck, a mass on the other lung would have had different conclusions entirely. Taking the facts in good stead, pneumonia and chest infections had caused weeks' stays in hospital, something Peter had hated. Child-like tantrums when informed that he wouldn't be discharged from the ward, all for his own good, caused intense discussions. He'd just wanted to be back home, where he belonged. All natural for every person living; home is where the heart is.

How Melinda had managed day after day driving to the hospital, staying with Peter for hours at a time, then going home to an empty house and bedtime, she hadn't known. Could she sleep? No chance, her head filled with what, when, where and what if! Meals consisted of food in the subway and Costa Coffee in the hospital, and snacks taken in to eat at Peter's bedside. A way of life, as it turned out. Problem after problem, the positivity was always there. Never giving up on life, both Peter and Melinda had stood firmly on the ground, hoping for a miracle.

Bingo had taken a back seat when Peter was in hospital, but now, today, Amanda and Melinda could please themselves as to when they could attend the leisure establishment, well, within reason anyway. The grandchildren had taken priority over certain days, the little angels that they were. Growing up so quickly, their needs were more important; missing watching them grow up was unthinkable. If Melinda was honest, life without them would be unimaginable. They were the future parents of their great grandchildren, and had required all the time their family could give them, with no excuses. Would she want it any other way? Absolutely not.

Melinda remembered herself as a naive eighteen year old, attending her first bingo session and establishment with her mother and her aunty Peggy, her mum's sister. She had hated it and couldn't understand where the enjoyment and enthusiasm had come into it. Melinda's mum was addicted to the game back in the day, when her five children were young. Any opportunity to visit the establishment she had taken, with one of her friends or alone.

Her dad had no interest in the game, he was more interested in having the odd flutter on the horses in the betting shop a few doors away. He was there to child mind Melinda and her four siblings at the time. Recalling her first experience of the game, her first visit, she could laugh at herself now.

Bingo was now her night out socialising, being with other like-minded people, whether they were known to each other or not. Regardless of any communication with any of them, the bingo hall was perfect entertainment and an excuse to fill their faces with a meal, a beverage (or alcohol if preferred) and a dessert, all at subsidised prices. So much cheaper than eating out in a public house or in a restaurant.

Melinda's youngest sister, still in primary school at the time, had written in her schoolbook about her previous day and evening, a kind of diary for the teachers to read. Each and every day, her first words written usually were "My mum went to bingo last night", before adding details of what she herself had done that evening or weekend. Melinda wondered what the teachers had thought at the time, but now, decades later, she was participating in the game nearly as much as her mother had. A guilty giggle had emerged from Melinda's mouth, a chuckle, and a cheeky smile.

Crossing off numbers called out by the host, in order to complete a line, two lines, and then a full house to secure a pay-out of monies if completing the game before anyone else. The game was simple enough and the rewards could be well worth winning. Melinda could shout "house" when required, not shy to have her voice heard any more.

Not exactly Las Vegas, the gambling paradise of the world, but equally entertaining for normal hard working people living on a budget. Monies lost, then won back, then lost again. If you were lucky, a few win wins before losing again. Swings and roundabouts really, but enthralling enough to continue visiting the bingo establishment.

Having visited Las Vegas twice in her lifetime, a place where there were even slot machines in the public conveniences; where you could order a meal and play a game of sudoku in the hope of a win to pay for their meals. Bingo halls in the UK had far to go to enable them to match the famous area known for its gambling twenty-four hours a day, but it had worked well enough for the majority of working class people around.

Melinda and Amanda had thoroughly enjoyed their weekly trip of an evening, usually on a Tuesday. A change for the better, a rest from humdrum days, and something to look forward to. Had Melinda ever thought that, after hating the game at eighteen, a mere teenager, she would now be following her mother's footsteps and liking the entertainment she had enjoyed years' ago? No, not in a million years. How peoples tastes and mannerisms change over the years.

If her mum had been alive today, the visits together would probably be more frequent than Melinda and Amanda's, much, much more. How Melinda had missed her mum now, and would willingly join her in the number crunching game that could bring good rewards. If only, if only! Just to hear her voice would have been absolutely wonderful.

Their evening out hadn't doubled the monies in their purses this time, unfortunately. It hadn't put either of them off though. Same again next week, both agreed with a positive nod. It was back to her home, alone. A cup of tea, a biscuit or two, and catching up on the soaps they had missed whilst being out. Bed followed and an attempt to sleep, which usually took hours.

She'd tried everything, a hot bath before bedtime infused with lavender oil, a hot milky drink, staying up late and later again. It hadn't happened, but maybe one day she just might fall to sleep quickly. Melinda persevered, looking at the alarm clock and her mobile phone on the bedside cabinet, then sighing when she'd seen the time; just an hour later than she'd last looked. One day sleepless nights would be a thing of the past, but for now, getting up late of a morning due to lack of sleep and total disinterest in life in general, Melinda's nights were normal to her and accepted for what they were.

Chapter Seven

Melinda had picked up her laptop the following day, retrieved her notebook and pen from the dining table, and continued looking for holidays again. Checking the previous travel areas and prices, she wanted to make a final choice and stick to it. She had felt a smidgen of confidence on getting up that morning, and had discussed vacations with Amanda a few days earlier.

Peter and Melinda had prepared a bucket list in their heads, and Ireland had been one of the countries they hadn't visited at all over the years. A few times, the country had been booked, only to be cancelled for some reason or another, she couldn't recall the actual facts now. Melinda's written list had included Ireland, with Dublin and Waterford as preferred locations. Peter had apologised to Melinda as he had become weaker, for not being able to fulfil their dreams. Ordinarily, before Peter had become ill, Melinda would have booked it, telling him afterwards of their next vacation.

A five day coach holiday was flagged up on the laptop, visiting Dublin and Waterford, and based in a place called Enniscorthy, a town in County Wexford. With Amanda's approval, she had booked the trip for the two of them in December, and paid the appropriate deposit. It was a few months' away yet, but finally Melinda had had something to look forward to. Peter would have huffed and puffed when told, but once away he would have relaxed and focused on the vacation, loving every minute of it. After forty-three years of marriage, she could read his mind perfectly, knowing full well that the break would have been thoroughly appreciated once the actual starting date had come.

Their last big holiday together, for their fortieth wedding anniversary, was a seven day coach break exploring the Canadian Rockies; followed by a seven day five star cruise to Alaska, then three days experiencing Vancouver in all its glory. A holiday Melinda had wanted to do, as long as her cancer hadn't ruined any chance of realising her dream escape. Peter had much preferred a sunny climate, always being a cold person externally. Their home would have the central heating on full blast, when the neighbours around were still basking outside in the sunshine.

He'd agreed to go though, to Canada and Alaska, for Melinda's sake. She would never ever forget their holiday of a lifetime; the timing being absolutely perfect. The following year, Peter had been diagnosed with terminal cancer, and three years of torment began. It had been everything and more; an experience never to be repeated. Melinda had no illusions there. They had witnessed it together, too many pictures in Melinda's head to share. The memories will never fade, not as long as she was still around.

Seeing a huge bear cross the road behind the coach, in the Rockies, was something neither of them had thought would ever happen. A husky ride in Alaska, through the woods and beyond, was exhilarating for Melinda. Peter had loved it, too. The Jacuzzi bath in their room, along with the balcony overlooking the glaciers of Alaska, was out of this world. Melinda had witnessed the dolphins swimming in two's towards the cruise liner, as she sat in the dining area drinking a hot chocolate one evening. Peter had missed seeing them. There were so many words to express the magical scenery around. It was awe-inspiring, beautiful, fantastic, glorious, and heaven on earth she'd supposed. If only Peter could tell Melinda what heaven was really like!

Melinda had decided to check out a months' vacation in the Canary Islands, being inquisitive about the costs involved, primarily. Both Peter and Melinda had spoken about his retirement from work, and wanting to travel more with their free time, when reaching the allotted future date. Several holidays in the sunshine, for more than the usual two weekly period was mentioned. With plenty of hours, days, and weeks to themselves, they were looking forward to planning where and when to go.

The final prices discovered, had Melinda pleasantly surprised. A one bedroomed bungalow in a holiday complex in Fuerteventura, an all-inclusive package, and not too far from the shops and the beach. Was it too good to be true? It had Melinda double checking everything she had submitted earlier. February was cold and miserable in the UK, but in Fuerteventura the sun shone daily. A good reason to swap the normal winter weather in Wales, for the sunshine in the Canary Islands. At an unexpectedly inexpensive price, it was too good to miss. Without thinking about it too much, Melinda had clicked the "book" button and paid the deposit requested.

Having never ventured on a solo vacation in her entire life, she had suddenly booked a twenty-eight day holiday to do exactly that, travel alone! Telling herself that she was doing it for herself and Peter had helped a little, and given her a reason for booking the long break. She had plenty of time to get used to the idea, months' in fact. Determined as she was, to Melinda this was a milestone to cross, and a hope of achieving goals set by her and her late husband.

Melinda had secretly laughed to herself, more of a giggle if she was honest. If she could do this, it would be the first step at being independent, something that would require a lot of confidence in herself. Not stupid, by any means, her lack of belief in being able to achieve things that were out of her comfort zone, was Melinda's failure. Now she was testing herself, there was absolutely no going backwards. She had no intention of letting Peter down either, this was doable, she could do it!

Another giggle, as Melinda thought about what Amanda would think of her, when telling her of her future plans. Her friend would never believe she would actually go ahead with the break, but Melinda wasn't going to give into failure, and knew that other plans would be required to complete her month away. An hotel to book for the evening before the flight. National Express tickets to Bristol bus station, and a bus to the airport. Finally, a call to her sister, hoping for a lift from the airport on return and a few days spent with her and her partner. In her head, Melinda had it all sorted out.

Amanda would think that her friend was mad, or worst. Melanie, her sister, probably the same. Melinda had no idea what her daughter would think about her mother's plans. Was she mad? Time would tell, one way or another. Why had she clicked on the "book" button? Reservations or not, Melinda now had two breaks to look forward to and closed the laptop after printing out the pages relevant to the holidays. A reason to be alive had just represented itself to her and there was plenty to organise in the future. A child had just come out of the sixty-three year old woman, Melinda, showing excitement rather than depression. All good, definitely worth a smile.

The local shop had required a visit. Melinda was out of milk and being unable to make herself a cup of tea wasn't something negotiable. It just couldn't happen. Peter wouldn't have been able to manage without his numerous cuppas every day. Melinda didn't drink so many, but hadn't wanted to run out of milk to prepare one. Cuppa after cuppa after cuppa, tea was Peter's nectar. He couldn't manage without tea.

Melinda had suddenly thought back to when she was a child, living next door to her grandmother, or Nan, as she was known. Her nan only ever used sterilised milk and cups of tea in her flat always tasted so different. Melinda had so enjoyed her cups of tea with her and keeping her company for an hour or two. She had died years ago, at the ripe old age of ninety-six. Melinda still missed her. Deciding to purchase some sterilised milk for a change, Melinda put on her coat and shoes, with her purse and a carrier bag in her hand as she walked out of the door.

With both sterilised and long-life milk purchased, a pack of two fresh cream chocolate eclairs which Melinda couldn't walk past, and a copy of the daily newspaper to read, she headed for Amanda's shop. Looking through the window to check whether she'd had a customer before entering, the bell had tinkled as she opened the door.

'Are you busy?' Melinda had asked her friend.

'I've a customer in half an hour, Mrs Thomas. You remember her, she remarried a year ago after losing her husband when she was really young. I can't recall her married name now, she will always be Mrs Thomas to me.' Amanda had rambled on before stopping abruptly. 'Is everything okay, Melinda?'

'Put the kettle on and I will tell you. I've got cream cakes to go with the tea.' Taking the eclairs from her carrier bag, she put them on the small table next to the two seater settee, there for Amanda's customers to feel at home whilst there.

Bringing the hot cups of tea from the small kitchenette, they ate their cakes quickly, the chocolate and cream forming around their lips. Sipping the hot liquid, Melinda informed her friend of the booked break to Ireland.

'I've paid the deposits for both of us. The remainder is due a month before we go.' Melinda had written the dates down for Amanda, as she would need to ensure that appointments were not made for those dates. 'I'm so looking forward to it.'

'Me too. I've never been to Ireland.' Amanda had responded.

'I've also booked another holiday, for me. I'm going to Fuerteventura in February, for a whole month.' Melinda waited for her friend's response.

Amanda had looked shocked, her grimace a picture. 'I will call around yours after work. You can fill me in on all the details then. I am shocked, but pleased for you. Who wouldn't want to spend a month in the sunshine, over a month here with the rain, coldness, and yet more rain.'

Her friend's customer had walked through the door, so Melinda made herself scarce. Picking up her carrier bag, she waved as she walked out, heading for home. A huge smile adorned her face, her suddenly energised body skipping all the way back to her house, well almost. Melinda had so much to organise now, she was going to be busy for the foreseeable future. It was something that she had so desperately needed at the moment.

Peter would have approved of Melinda's decision to travel, pursuing their dreams on her own or with friends. He wouldn't have wanted her to wallow in self-pity, even though at times she was doing just that. The tears still fell, especially at night when nobody could see her. The evening before, late at night, a pretty brown and red butterfly was flying around the living room swiftly. From wall to wall, bashing into the television, the gas fire, then back again. Melinda had no issues with it, letting it fly around without even trying to catch it, but had wondered where it had come from. Was it a message from Peter?

Melinda's mum was very superstitious, and she herself had followed in her mother's footsteps, most of the time. Not walking underneath a ladder was common sense in itself, and also very logical, but Melinda never did walk underneath one purely for its superstition. Not putting new shoes on a table, or cutting her toenails on a Thursday, were superstitions that hadn't anything sense-like about them. Melinda always followed them, though. Not putting an umbrella up in the house, throwing salt over your left shoulder if spilled, were others she could recall. There were a lot of others, too. Not marrying in May, or on a Friday, supposedly bad luck; superstitions not always adhered to.

Her mum had married in May, the first time, and Melinda's daughter had married on a Friday and in May, just two years ago. Marry in May and rue the day, the saying goes. Melinda had remembered it well. The saying had originated back to Ancient Rome. It was considered a bad omen because

May was the month of the Feast of the Dead, and three days of that month was devoted to cleansing the evil dead spirits. It appears the society frowned upon couples seeking to get married, thus making their union unlucky because they were meant to be paying homage to the deceased.

Melinda recalled other superstitions buried deep in her mind. A broken mirror being bad luck (she always kept a small piece of mirror for seven years to avoid the bad luck), crossing knives at the dining table or when washing up, Bird poop was known to bring good fortune, and a pure black cat crossing the road in front of you could mean you were cursed, or, in Pirates theory the black cat was lucky unless it turned away from you, which then became a bad omen.

Melinda had hoped and prayed that her youngest grandson wasn't born on a Wednesday, or on the date of her mum's funeral a year earlier. Thankfully he had arrived on a Thursday, in between the two dates. Thursday's child has far to go; a definition of her youngest grandson, he has always been a bright boy, showing signs of good intelligence. He is also part of the bolt that keeps Melinda, his grandmother, together. He keeps her sane with his mentions of his granddad, his innocence laughable, but acknowledging Granddad's existence is so, so crucial. A five year old hitting all the right notes!

Wednesday's child is full of woe, as the saying goes. Melinda's daughter was born on a Wednesday, and her life so far hadn't been easy, by any means. Friday the thirteenth had Melinda playing her day as low key as possible. Fear of something horrific happening on the day; better to be safe than sorry. The 1st of April had held a poignant day in her head. Pinch punch, the 1st of the month, a time to fool others before noon usually, but for Melinda it had represented the date the hospital had informed her of her breast cancer diagnosis, nine years earlier. A date never to forget, chance would be a fine thing.

As Melinda opened the door to her home, the smile was still there. Look before you leap had suddenly come to mind, but was dismissed very quickly. She was certain that she was doing the right thing, there wasn't any doubt at all. Glancing around the living room for the butterfly of yesterday, she'd found it hanging on the wall. Picking it up and allowing it to fly away outside, it had nestled on the grass before doing just that.

Chapter Eight

Melinda had purchased some flowers in her local Lidl store, yellow carnations to be exact. They were to put on Peter's gravestone in the church her daughter had married in, two years earlier. She hadn't religiously visited the grave, it was more as and when, where she was concerned. In the cold winter weather, Melinda had put artificial flowers down, not wanting to venture to the memorial ground in the cold and the rain.

Peter had expressed his wishes to his daughter before his passing. He had told her to lay his ashes somewhere, and visit him once a year; not on his birthday, as they were always different days of the week. Preferably on Father's Day, as it would always be on a Sunday. Melinda had no idea where that had come from, but as he hadn't spoken directly to her, she hadn't adhered to it herself.

Fresh flowers were carefully positioned regularly by Melinda, she wasn't a flower arranger though, but did the best she could. The church was local to Melinda's daughter's home, so travelling to the grave wasn't out of her way. Picking up her youngest grandson from school, followed by going to visit her husband, then back to her daughter's, had broken her day up. She had felt gratified that it was a journey

Melinda could do easily. The crematorium would have been a lot harder for her to achieve, being much further away.

'Hello Granddad,' the sweet five year old would say, looking towards the sky. Then turning towards his grandma he would utter 'Can Granddad phone us?'

Being so hard to explain death to a youngster, he was confused as to why his granddad wasn't with Melinda now. 'Can Granddad see us?' and 'How far up in the sky is heaven?' followed by 'If Granddad is better now, why can't he come back down from heaven?' Melinda loved hearing him recall Peter, asking questions, and knowing he had loved his granddad dearly. He would never forget him, Melinda knew.

Thinking back to her own mother's passing, six years ago now, a decision as to where to scatter her ashes had Melinda and her siblings pondering on an agreed spot. Melinda's mother had lost her own mum (Melinda's grandmother) when she was just eleven years of age. Ada was working on the farm the day before, the tied cottage being owned by the farmer. It had been a condition when renting the cottage, that either Ada or Harry (Melinda's grandfather) needed to work on the farm in exchange for paying a rental agreement.

Ada would milk the cows, help out with the harvesting, and tend to the vegetable plot. She had enjoyed it and hadn't thought of it as a chore; all her life, even as a child, helping her dad in the fields was normal for her. Harry had had a job in the nearest town as a steamroller driver, a job he had loved. Also used to living on a farm, he'd spent his childhood doing chores for his grandparents. He had lived with them from birth until he'd joined the army at twenty years old.

The following day, Ada hadn't felt well and a doctor was called to the cottage. She'd deteriorated as the day went on and died later in the evening. She was just thirty-eight years old, and left three confused children and Harry, her husband, behind. Refusing to take over his wife's roll on the farm, they were made homeless. Temporarily, they moved in with an army friend and his wife and son, not far from their cottage.

The children were all separated, two sisters and a brother, Melinda's mother moving in with her step-grandmother and grandfather, before moving in with a favourite aunty and uncle a few years later. Harry remained with his army friend for a while, before becoming "a gentleman of the road." Melinda's mum had lived with her cousin, as sisters, and they were always close. Her mother's uncle had passed away a long time ago, followed by her aunty years' later. Their son had passed away at a young age, in his early twenties, very suddenly.

Asking her cousin as to where to scatter her mother's ashes, she had wanted Melinda's mum to be included in the family grave, dedicated to the three of them and soon to be four. Melinda and her siblings agreed with the decision, apart from Melinda's youngest sister, who had wanted her ashes spread in the small village churchyard that had been the family's home until Ada's death. Amelia was now resting with the people she had loved, with a small granite plaque bearing her full name and age, in the village churchyard in Chew Magna, local to the cottage she had lived with her mother's sister and her family. Flowers were placed on the grave regularly, for all to see.

Having visited the rural village in Somerset, a place called Norton St Philip, a civil parish in the Mendip district, Melinda had understood her mother's love of the area whilst growing up. As a child of four years of age, Amelia remained there until her own mother's death, and even moving around with her grandfather and step-grandmother was well within the boundaries of Norton St Philip. She stopped moving from house to house, and relative to relative, in her twenties; in her sister's house in the city of Bristol. The next door neighbour's son had taken a shine to her, and they eventually married and started their own family, Melinda being the eldest of her children.

The small community was quaint and quiet, and had felt homely immediately. The two public houses, opposite one another, had historical backgrounds going back centuries. Popular for their pub food and bed and breakfast rooms, Melinda's mum had spoken about her life around the village before her death; Melinda could envisage her and her sister sat on the steps of the local public house, disobeying Ada's orders not to be there. Amelia, as a child, wasn't always good, a bit of a rebel in her time it had appeared.

The day of Amelia's funeral, in Bristol, should have been a break to Norton St Philip with Melinda and her younger sister. Recapturing their mother's childhood, with Amelia there to show them; recalling her happy, carefree years there. It wasn't to be, but with the cottage booked for two nights, Melinda and Peter had travelled to the area afterwards to view the place Melinda's mother had spoken of, staying in the cottage, but without Melinda's mother. Melanie and her partner had joined them on the second day. The description of the tied cottage, opposite the police house, amid the farmland Ada had worked, had Melinda focusing on finding it. The farmland was now occupied with expensive houses, but the area was named after the farm that was there years gone by. Melinda could imagine her mother happily living there with her siblings.

Her father, Harry, would walk the few steps to the local public house, the Fleur de Llys, for his two pints of cider. Peter and Melinda had enjoyed an alcoholic beverage there on the first evening, sat on a table overlooking the pretty village. Melinda could envisage her grandfather sitting there, with his pipe and glass of cider, revelling in the quiet and solitude. A loner, Harry was more than content with his own company.

Having found the church, and the churchyard, they tried to find any stone or marker indicating Ada and Harry, and Vera, their youngest daughter's existence. There was nothing, but having spoken to the vicar of the church, she was able to pinpoint where their ashes were buried. A stone in remembrance of the family that had lived there was required, and Melinda had spent weeks when home, sorting one out. Months' later, a stone was put in place, not only mentioning the three people laid there, but also recognising Melinda's mum, her mum's sister, and her brother; all now reunited in heaven.

Melinda and Peter had visited Norton St Philip several times after that, placing flowers on the stone, and enjoying the area and its natural beauty. Their fortieth wedding anniversary was spent in the Fleur de Llys with siblings and cousins, after returning from their holiday of a lifetime in Canada and Alaska. Sadly, she wouldn't be able to visit again, with Peter now joining others in heaven. Such a shame, but life had a tendency of changing things. Not always for the better, either!

Having done her duty for the day, Melinda drove back to her home. She hadn't eaten all day again, and was feeling slightly dizzy. Food was required, a much deserved cup of tea, and another evening sat on the sofa watching the soaps. There were chores to be done, or finished, but she had to want to do certain things and catch up on some energy to achieve her goals. Mostly, and at the moment, Melinda hadn't the get-up-and-go to catch up on housework and the like.

She wasn't being lazy, Melinda had told herself, but inwardly she was cussing; knowing she could manage, but actually managing was two different things altogether. Arthritis throughout her body over the years, normally caused more severe issues in the colder weather. Her hands refused to do what her head had ordered her to. Sometimes, her grip became impossible and picking objects up was well out of the question. The stick grabber had helped her then, but not until Melinda had tried several times using her hands before giving up completely.

General hoovering and dusting wasn't done daily; it was only her own mess that required dealing with. Living alone, she had discovered that the washing machine wasn't used on a daily basis; twice a week was more than adequate. Likewise, the stick hoover only needed using a couple of times a week, at the most. As for the dusting, well, Melinda ignored it the majority of the time, pretending it wasn't there. Her attitude towards keeping the house in order, had changed considerably from her younger days. Even when bringing the children up and working part-time, the house was always spic and span, with nothing out of place, ever.

Recalling her mother, Amelia, as she had gotten older, Melinda was definitely following in her footsteps. Never one to be house-proud, with five children and a husband around, it was almost impossible in any case. Melinda remembered her chores as a teenager; the stairs needed brushing down, two flights of them, cleaning the bedroom she shared with her two sisters, and washing the dishes after Sunday lunch. Sunday evening, she would iron all the washed clothes for the seven of them; all packed neatly into piles for each individual person concerned. Did she continue ironing her clothes on a Sunday? Not a chance, Melinda ironed only what was necessary, and nothing else.

With a microwave meal prepared, a cup of tea, both placed on a lap-tray, Melinda carried them into the living room and put the television on. The local news was on whilst she had eaten her food, all pretty boring really. The soaps were on afterwards, so she settled herself down to watch them. Closing the curtains, hiding the dark skies from view, the dirty dishes could wait until tomorrow morning. Amelia would have scolded her for neglecting her duties, Melinda could see her face now, an angry grimace so recognisable; but he-ho, she hadn't concerned herself about a few pieces of crockery.

Picking up her paperwork regarding the booked holidays a few days earlier, after the soaps had finished that was, Melinda scanned the details and wrote a separate page of the to do's to finalise all the arrangements needed. There was a hotel attached to the airport in Bristol, quite a pricey one, but it was convenient and she knew a date had required booking there, to safeguard her plans. National Express, and a bus from Bristol bus station to the airport, something else requiring a confirmed booking. Although the month long holiday was months' away, Melinda's methodical dealings ensured all was done and dusted as early as conveniently possible. How different she was to dusting the house! She had laughed at herself just thinking about it.

The five day vacation to Ireland was all sorted, except for taking a trip to a travel agent to obtain some Euros. The break wasn't that far away, the beginning of December. Melinda was happy about everything on that score. Amanda was so looking forward to the break, as was Melinda. Her friend had laughed about Melinda's booking to Fuerteventura, and still wasn't convinced that she would actually go through with the holiday planned. Peter had come to mind, just then. She was doing it for both of them and was determined to see the long break through. She did have an ulterior motive, to take her lap-top and finish writing her novel started whilst nursing Peter. It had been put on hold what with everything going on. Melinda wanted to finish it whilst enjoying the sunshine as well. She could try, anyway!

An early night was out of the question, there was absolutely no point in it. A Christmas film was showing on the movies channel, very early, but a simple and relaxing film to entertain her mind. Her evenings had been mapped out for her, something not requiring much thought or too much action to her lazy brain. Tomorrow would be a different day altogether, but probably pretty much of the same. With the gas fire and central heating on, Melinda wondered if Peter was cold, wherever he was now. She hadn't wanted him to feel cold and hoped he liked the fresh flowers she had put in place earlier that day.

Chapter Nine

Peter was a plasterer by trade, having undertaken as a job for over thirty years. Previous to that he had spent over twenty years working in an aluminium foundry, remaining there until the foundry in question had closed down. It was after that, that Peter, Melinda, and the children had moved from Bristol to Wales. He had wanted to work outside, from building to building, doing manual work, rather than being enclosed constantly in one building for a full working day.

Being taken seriously by a company in Wales, his years in the building trade had begun. Peter loved what he was doing, out in the fresh air and travelling from house to house renovating people's properties. It was hard work, not brilliantly paid, but meeting owners needing jobs done to their homes, and receiving praise for his work was reward enough.

If the owners had kept him and his workmates in cups of tea and biscuits, a happy person he was, regardless of how much work had been required. Melinda would hear about his day most evenings. Knowing the residents by name whilst working on their premises, the elderly ladies seemed to adore him, often preparing sandwiches for Peter at lunchtime, and cakes of various types piled onto a plate for him and his workmates to savour. All were consumed with endless cups of sweetened tea. A lunch box was always taken with him every morning, and the contents were eaten as well. Peter should have put on weight, and tripled his actual body mass shown on the bathroom scales. But with all the fattening food scoffed each and every day, Peter's framework always replicated a slim figure. Way too skinny for his five foot and ten inches stature.

Inherited or not, cake and chocolate hadn't remained in the kitchen cupboards for long. Chance would be a fine thing, if the grandsons were around as well. When the bread van used to stop outside the house selling their wares, Peter would be there purchasing custard slices, chocolate and cream eclairs, and jam doughnuts. A child savouring a sweet treat with pure delight, his excitement should have been caught in a photograph for all to see.

Peter had loved his work, perfecting everything he had put his heart into, and when returning home, the work hadn't stopped. Whether it was improving their own residence or his son's or daughter's homes, he carried on until it was time to go to bed of an evening. If he wasn't doing something inside the home or the children's houses, or a neighbour's property, it was the garden being tended to; the vegetable plot weeded or watered and produce being picked for consumption. Peter was never idle, not until his health had taken a turn for the worst, and he had been unable to muster up any energy to achieve anything at all.

Melinda had recalled her husband telling her that he couldn't carry on his work in the building trade, probably months' before his diagnosis had hailed its ugly head. The words spoken by the consultant had hit home, hard. Having gone through the big 'C' herself, how cruel was it to hear that her husband was indeed suffering from the big 'C' too. What had either of them done to deserve it? Peter had taken it calmly, if Melinda was honest. Doctors and nurses were astounded; sometimes overcome with how well he had taken and laughed off procedures with a joke or two.

'I'm thinking the worst and hoping for the best,' he had told a nurse after having a biopsy in his lung. 'My wife has breast cancer,' he had added very matter of fact. Knowing her husband well enough, Melinda knew he was covering up his own worries with a light-hearted front. Was he concerned for his health? Of course he was.

It hadn't all been doom and gloom though. Yes, the hospital appointments were frequent, the chemotherapy horrific. The radiotherapy was a never-ending trip after trip to the hospital for treatment; but in between the lows of everything, Peter savoured precious memories with Melinda and the family. Visiting family members in Bristol and friends in Devon, he was still able to drive until the very end, and made the most of his time.

Holiday breaks were managed between treatments, and even one year before the cancer had won over his tired body, he was helping Melinda's brother and sister-in-law with pulling the kitchen to pieces for Melinda and Peter's updated version in the most used room in the house. It was the last room in their home to be given a modern update, or a fresh coat of paint, something Melinda's husband had wanted to achieve before he'd left the earth, knowing his wife would be okay without him. He had hated watching others do a job he should have been able to do on his own, and so wanted to join in with the eventual completion, some months later. Fatigue wouldn't let him, unfortunately.

Peter was adored by everyone who knew him, well almost. He hadn't a bad bone in his body, or a bad word to say about anyone, well again, almost! Had he deserved to suffer at the end? Absolutely not, but none of us can choose how we end our days, it was something completely out of our control. Hindsight should teach us not to get into bad habits; not to smoke cigarettes or drink alcohol too heavily. Would that ensure good health throughout our years? No, not necessarily. Moderation, everything in moderation. Even that wouldn't guarantee a long and carefree existence for anyone. Melinda's husband had drawn the short straw, but every day of his life lived represented a memory for Melinda and the family, one to be so grateful for.

Peter, as well as Amelia, Melinda's mum, had a few idiosyncrasies that would cause a giggle or two at times; a smile at remembering certain things done in the past. As a new and proud father to their son, Peter's effort at changing the baby's nappy was useless. On picking up the baby afterwards, the terry towelling nappy and fastening pin fell to the floor through his tiny legs. Plop! It had hit the carpet at high speed. He never changed a nappy after that, just recalling his careful movements, his utter patience, and the result, had Melinda in stitches. It was so funny and something recalled for its relevance; Peter had so wanted to help out.

Even in dire circumstances, Melinda never allowed him to change either of the children's nappies again. On getting their son ready to go out for a ride in the car, with slightly damp socks taken from the clothes airer, Peter's brainwave to dry the tiny socks quickly was to put them under the grill. They melted into a nice mess on the base of the grill pan, which took hours to clean off afterwards. Melinda had laughed out loud, often reminding him of his error and thought process at the time.

Watching Peter attempt to dress Thomas or Stephanie in a baby-grow was hilarious, the poppers were always snapped into the wrong place, causing gaps and obsolete poppers on the piece of baby wear used when children were tiny. Melinda would huff and puff, rearranging and correcting her husband's effort at fatherhood. Now, years later, Peter's mishaps when the children were tiny, were happy talking points. He was good at picking Thomas, their son, up during the night, and pacing up and down the bedroom when he was teething and unable to sleep, something he undertook without question. He loved his children, at whatever ages they were.

Not a natural born gardener, Peter had carefully dug flowers from their small backyard and replanted them into his sister's flower border in her garden, pleased with his efforts. Days later, his sister had realised that Peter had actually planted weeds into her garden. It became a laughing conversation at their father's home for weeks and weeks. Peter was never allowed to forget it!

Peter's father, a bricklayer by trade, had built a high garden wall to stop his grandson from entering the pedestrian lane and refraining him from entering a busy main road. He had made a good job of it, too. Peter's job was to erect a garden gate with a childproof bolt on it, sufficient enough to deter a two year old boy. Pleased with his handy work, they left Thomas in the garden to play, only to find their son had climbed the gate and was playing in the lane. Good job, Peter!

His role at Christmas Eve, was to quietly take the children's stockings up and put them at the base of their beds. As he walked up the stairs shouting Ho Ho Ho, they had instantly woken up as he returned downstairs. The presents were opened promptly before their parents had even went to bed. Peter had loved Christmas when the children were younger, he had become a child himself.

Peter couldn't spell if his life had depended on it. Mobile phones and televisions should never break down, he couldn't adjust to anything new. His brain would go into overdrive and he would cuss and cuss having to learn new techniques; he always did get used to the new devises eventually, but not out of choice. If it's not broke then why fix it! The phrase could have been written by him, if he could spell the words, that was. During his illness Peter would text their daughter daily, and she would respond if she had understood the text. Melinda would laugh at his spelling mistakes, but commended him for at least trying.

He was always losing something, usually it was his mobile phone or the car or house keys. Hours were wasted finding one or the other, leaving two heads fretting and going over and over Peter's last movements in order to find the lost item or items. Where had he left them?

His teeth were the most annoying part of his body; always falling out at the most inappropriate times. His front tooth had fallen out on their Alaskan cruise, when celebrating their fortieth wedding anniversary. Keeping the tooth safe, Peter tried not to smile too often. On disembarking the ship and being booked into a hotel in Vancouver for three days, their first place of visit, after speaking to the receptionist for addresses and directions, was to a dentist and having the tooth temporarily glued in place. Both Melinda and Peter could totally recommend the dentists in Vancouver, Canada. They well outshone dentists in the UK for their hospitality, cleanliness, and five star dental surgeries. Melinda could bet (and win) that no-one else on a holiday of a lifetime would have paid a visit to a dentist as part of their itinerary.

On several occasions, whilst abroad, his teeth would fall out without any warning. When holidaying in Tenerife, when eating out, UK destinations were not eliminated either. Even at home, after having a tooth re-stuck; his first bite of food, followed by a look of concern as he'd swallowed the evidence and booked yet another visit to the dentist. Everyone around the dining table had tried not to laugh, but hadn't succeeded in keeping the grimaces from him. Dentists wouldn't have reaped a lot of money where Peter's mouth was concerned. His teeth, or lack of them, were a constant talking point when mentioning the dental practice. Peter had taken it all in good humour, but in reality it wasn't a laughing matter.

Being a smoker of cigarettes since his teenage years, he had taken his lung cancer diagnosis appropriately. A sign of the times, Peter's younger years had a lot of people in his vicinity taking up the habit. It was the done thing in his day, following his mates in smoking the nicotine stick. When Melinda had been told of her breast cancer diagnosis, it was a shock to him, she had never smoked cigarettes in her lifetime, and never would. Being unable to strike a match or hold a lighter for fear of the flame itself, the thought had never crossed her mind.

He had stopped the habit a few times, putting on weight without the cigarettes, weight that had needed to be there; the odd crafty one would be smoked in Amanda's house, with Melinda not knowing. Whenever Melanie was around, a smoker since her teenage years, Melinda knew that one or two would pass his lips when she was out of sight. Peter had blamed himself for his illness, but in all honesty lung cancer wasn't always a result of smoking cigarettes. He'd just been unlucky, and smoking hadn't helped the condition.

After Peter's passing, Melinda had been looking for something in the shed, and opened a tin box discovering several empty packets of tobacco, some green papers, and cigarette stubs. The damage had already been done, and all Melinda could do was laugh to herself before replacing the tin box where she had found it. He had smoked several secretive cigarettes, even at the end. The crafty so-and-so, Melinda had giggled again. Peter was Peter for all his bad habits, and Melinda had loved him regardless of all of them. Looking to the sky, she'd wondered whether he was continuing his habit in heaven? With his wit, he was probably singing and dancing, too.

Amelia would probably be there with him, Melinda could visualise them both up to no good. She would be there, in the kitchen, ensuring he had a hearty dinner in him every day. Peter had been so looking forward to a pub meal, a well done steak and chips; onion rings, mushrooms, peas, all the trimmings. He had waited patiently for his operation on his throat, a side effect of his chemotherapy and radiotherapy, hoping his voice and his ability to swallow would return. Sadly, the swallowing hadn't returned and he was being fed via a tube in his stomach, only allowed to sip water to keep his lips moist. His voice had returned, but not to its normal singing pitch.

Melinda's five year old grandson had so wanted to find that four-leaf clover, wishing his granddad back from heaven. Melinda, herself, would have instantly ordered him a plate full of the steak, chips, and extras that he had so thrived for. When eating out, she couldn't bring herself to eat a main meal incorporating steak, chips and the trimmings. Peter wouldn't have minded at all, she was certain, but it hadn't felt right when Melinda's husband had so looked forward to demolishing the so wanted platter of food.

Peter's eldest sister, if she was now with them, would have frowned on her baby brother's frolicking about. When aunty Pat was around, the siblings would all bow to her (when on holiday together), all in jest really. Being the eldest of the five of them, they all tried to behave around her, try being the operative word!

Chapter Ten

Friends, Melinda's head had recalled the many people Peter and Melinda had found, doing what they had both loved, travelling. Some remained on the Christmas card list, whilst others bonded as almost family relatives, true friendship going over and above their calling. How crucial they were at this moment in time, she'd rambled on in her brain, remembering so many happy thoughts. She was so lucky to have met so many lovely people on their endless travels.

Telephone conversations had occurred often, some more frequent than others, but catching up on one another's comings and goings was an occasion to smile down the receiver, the majority of the time, that was. There would be bad news, losing loved ones to illnesses and some so suddenly that neither Peter nor Melinda could believe the news. Newly born grandchildren, adding to their family, was always welcomed. Holidays gone and upcoming leisure trips booked, the globe was visited by almost all the friends making the connection. Life was all about doing the best they could with the funds they had, and mostly being middle aged or older, whether their health could indeed manage their individual goals.

Reginald and Mary were two such people who, after enjoying a week long coach holiday to Scotland, based at Fort William, became firm family members though not blood related at all. Melinda had offered them both a strawberry and cream flavoured sweet on the coach, and from then there was no turning back. With an invitation to Mary's fiftieth birthday get-together at their home in Devon, holidays and meeting up at each other's homes became frequent, despite the distance. They were there to help out when Melinda was going through her breast cancer, taking her away with them to Cornwall for a weeks' vacation, and relieving Peter and Stephanie from their caring duties for a much needed break. She would always be grateful for their help.

Peter, as always, was the child on the coach; singing along to the song Alice, and including the swear word always associated with it, quite a strong expletive. The Belgian band, there to visit their families in Scotland, looked on at Peter, continuing playing the song with gusto. When they played Auld Lang Syne, Peter promptly got everyone in the lounge area of the hotel up, joining hands and singing the end of year song, in the middle of April! The devil in him, had everyone singing Happy Birthday to You to Mary, when it wasn't even her birthday. Peter would never be forgotten on their Scottish holiday, for all the wrong reasons.

A visit to Stirling Bridge, had Peter running across it, carrying his invisible sword and replicating the Scottish knight Sir William Wallace who was famous for being one of the main leaders during the First War of Scottish Independence; Wallace defeated an English army at the battle of Stirling Bridge in September 1297. On August the fifth 1305, he was arrested near Glasgow and taken to London, where he was hanged, disembowelled, beheaded, and quartered. Needless to say, Reginald was Robert 1, more commonly known as Robert the Bruce, King of Scotland from 1306 to his death in 1329. With the two of them acting out the battle, who needed children!

Melinda still managed to visit and stay with them for a break, now alone, catching the National Express coaches, and Reginald picking her up in Exeter. A drive through Dartmoor, admiring the wild horses, various breeds of cattle and sheep, and the ponies. Beautiful scenery passing by before crossing the hairy hand bridge, where legend has it that the hairy hand would catch the vehicle before throwing it into the water. Jay's grave, where fresh flowers were placed each and every day without fail, but it's still a mystery as to who puts them there. A ghostly figure has been seen near there, by others; Melinda had never seen it, though.

Several holidays had been shared by the two couples, in beautiful areas of the country. The Isle of Wight was visited twice, once with the addition of Amelia, Melinda's mother, and her cousin Sylvia. Both times were memorable, but with Amelia and Sylvia there, the song by Tina Turner called Simply the Best has hysterical memories. Mary and Sylvia dancing to the song had tears of laughter streaming from everyone's eyes, those in the holiday party. Good fun was had by all, the whole reason for breaks away from a daily regime in life. It was just what the doctor had ordered!

Playing a game of bingo in the lounge of the hotel, for a box of assorted biscuits, was the highlight of one evening in the Isle of Wight. A second night there became the floor for ballroom dancers, something none of them could do. Watching a gentleman, who was totally blind, sliding elegantly around the dance floor with his wife, had put the four of them to shame. He was so graceful, perfect footings for a human being that was living totally in the dark. All eyes were upon the couple, applauding them as the music ended.

Fishguard, on the Pembrokeshire coast, became a regular holiday park visited. Just Melinda and Peter at times, and including Reginald and Mary on other dates, the coastal area with the stunning views around it, was enjoyed for its beauty and friendliness. The caravan's entertainment club was small in contrast to bigger sites, but feeling completely at home there, Melinda could happily enter the building on her own and totally relax. Regulars to the site became friends whilst there, all speaking to each other as if they'd known each other for years.

Home from home, with a game of bingo and cabaret entertainment thrown in. A mug of tea as a drink from the bar was prepared by the bar staff without any fuss. A service provided without anyone batting an eyelid. The daily quizzes usually had Peter and Melinda coming last, recognising the fact each and every time, but still joining in with the fun. Melinda's husband had loved it there, he'd joined in with anything thrown at him, and generally devoured the ambience of the caravan park as a whole. She so missed the place herself, if Melinda was being honest.

A couple that Melinda and Peter had met in America, whilst spending two weeks in a place called Laughlin, known as the mini Las Vegas, were initially on their Christmas card list, but later became telephone buddies as well as exchanging letters from time to time. Booking a caravan in Great Yarmouth one year, and another in Kings Lynn a few years later, they were able to meet them and spend time being with each other again. Their home address in the county of Norfolk, enabled the meet ups thoroughly appreciated by all four adults.

With an almost identical pattern of life's ups and downs, it appeared quite daunting when conversing with them both. Peter and John had hired a boat on the Norfolk Broads for a few hours. Taking it in turns to steer the boat, they had concentrated on the task at hand. Aye, Aye Captain! Linda and Melinda would catch up on each other's lives happily seated at the back of the smallish boat. The similarity of life's sequences was uncanny, surreal even.

Linda had discovered her breast cancer diagnosis after returning from America, Graceland to be exact. Thankfully, she had beat it, now completely rid of the invasive disease in her body. John had then become ill himself, years later, suffering from breathing difficulties. Sadly, he'd passed away not long ago, leaving Linda completely bereft without her husband and best friend.

Peter and Melinda's lives appeared to duplicate theirs. Melinda had also been diagnosed with breast cancer after travelling to Graceland, the home of the King, Elvis Presley. She too, had beat it and was still here. Peter, at first showing breathing difficulties, before being diagnosed with lung cancer, had passed away too. Melinda's mood was almost identical to her friend's, lost without their partners. They would remain telephone and letter writing friends, but being so far away distance-wise, the chance of meeting up again was verging on the impossible.

Brian and Andrea, residing in Bradford, West Yorkshire, had met Melinda and Peter on a Greek holiday, Corfu, she recalled. Conversation began whilst sat on the sandy beach, in the glorious sunshine. Arranging to meet up in one of the tavernas for a meal and a drink, the four of them continued sharing their evenings together throughout their holiday. Had Peter managed to make people take notice of him whilst there? Had he made a spectacle of himself? Of course he had!

A bus trip to the town itself had got them there easily enough. Unbeknown to them, Corfu town, especially the old part of it, was a maze of cobbled streets with shops galore both sides. So much to see and buy, eating and drinking in cafes outside on the street itself. All so enchanting, historical buildings being used to sell their wares with seating areas to take in the gorgeous scenery. Somehow, they had managed to find the bus stop in time for the return journey back to their hotel. The bus was almost full and they needed to keep track of where they were heading. The hotel wasn't visible from the road, with the complex built on the coast, deep in a valley. Five flights of steps were needed climbing, to reach the main road itself, and breathing stops were required when going up and down them.

Peter was keeping an eye on the road, or so Melinda had thought. As the bus continued past their stop, he had suddenly recognised certain markers and stood up abruptly. It was too late for the driver to stop, so they had both exited the bus in a place called Kassiopi. They hadn't a clue as to how they were to get back to their holiday location, but as they were there, Melinda and Peter checked out the area and the awe-inspiring marina. A soft drink enjoyed taking in the scenery and suddenly they had both fallen in love with it. As the daylight had suddenly turned into evening, the only way to return to their complex was to flag a taxi down, which they had managed easily enough.

As if it was meant to happen, Andrea and Brian had been walking, as the bus passed them. They both noticed Peter stood up in the aisle, and had wondered why he hadn't got off. That evening, around one of the tavernas overlooking the beach, Peter had had every one of them in hysterics. Only Melinda's husband could cause so much laughter, but, on the plus side they had found a place to holiday in the future. Kassiopi became a vacation stayed in for a one or two weeks' break, three times in their lifetime. Coincidence, or not, they had bumped into their neighbours back home. Living opposite them, how good it was to see familiar faces on their two weeks' away from their UK residence.

Andrea and Brian became more than Christmas card companions. Letters and photographs were exchanged; their eldest daughter's wedding photograph in Australia and their youngest daughter's in Bradford. Always wanting to visit them at some time in the future, sadly it never happened. The Christmas card keeps on coming, year after year, bringing fond memories of the memorable holiday in Corfu and lovely people met there.

It was in Kassiopi that Melinda had booked an hours' horse riding experience. Why she had done it, she'd no clue. Neither of them had ever rode a horse before, Peter often backed them in the bookmakers, that was as far as either of them had ventured in that field. As Melinda had walked up to the horse she would be riding, the nerves had gotten the better of her. Was she mad? With the help of the men and women employed there, Melinda sat on her horse and was then given a stick to hit the horse's bottom with. She didn't want to hit it and couldn't see why she would have to. As the pack of horses with their riders (that was debatable) trotted away, Melinda's horse wouldn't move. She was ordered to hit it with her stick, and had no choice but to adhere to orders given.

Thirty minutes riding through the olive trees, a short break for refreshments, then thirty minutes riding along the sandy beach. Would she want to do it again, or Peter, for that matter? No, but they had both achieved something different, way out of their comfort zone. They both had photographs to prove it, too. Melinda's bucket list included having a ride on an elephant, something she has yet to accomplish. She will do it, when, she'd no idea but it was there in her head yet to have at least tried.

Peter's karaoke singing had brought with it friendly companions for the short time visiting the area. An evening crammed with listening to others sing their heart out, or at least trying to. Melinda's husband had loved the atmosphere karaoke nights had delivered. He transformed himself into somebody else, singing his Elvis Presley songs to complete strangers, without a care in the world. Enjoyment was what it was all about and he excelled himself on that score. Melinda would sit and listen whilst enjoying an alcoholic beverage, smiling and applauding him. If they had returned to their hotel before twelve o'clock midnight, then something was terribly wrong. It hadn't happened though, they had become naughty children creeping back home in the early hours of the morning. Except they weren't children, just adults entertaining themselves, a brilliant reward for their hard earned monies and living the dream. All good, who could think otherwise!

Chapter Eleven

There were certain members of the family that had, throughout Melinda and Peter's illnesses, gone over and above the call of duty. There to help in various capacities; cooking, cleaning, a shoulder to cry on when needed, and just being around them. A definite help when going through regimes of treatment, and suffering side effects, incapable of attending to day to day chores through sheer fatigue. Ironing clothes, using the steam iron, Melinda couldn't muster up any encouragement to even try to achieve something that was so normal.

Melanie, Melinda's sister, was one of those people. A three or four day break from her home in Bristol, she would cook most meals, clean around and tackle the ever mounting pile of unironed clothes. Peter had seemed to light up on her arrival, loved her being there, and looked forward to the meals that she had concocted from the food in the fridge and pantry cupboard. A drive to a public house for a meal, Peter would make the effort to take her and Melinda somewhere along the Welsh coast when she was with them.

At times, it would be after a hospital appointment, the drive around the scenic coast not far from the hospital itself; Melanie would go with them to the hospital, remaining in the waiting area until Peter and Melinda had seen whichever consultant was required at the time. On one occasion, with Peter worse for wear after chemotherapy and Melinda having somehow contracted shingles, Melanie had caught the National Express coach, or James had driven her to theirs (Melinda couldn't quite remember), and she had taken over the household chores, leaving both of them to rest and recover.

Amelia had, on several occasions, suffered from shingles, but it wasn't until Melinda had actually been diagnosed with it herself, did she realise the true extent of the illness. She couldn't cope with everyday things she had taken for granted, or the pain and worn out feeling that were the makings of shingles. Melanie herself had also suffered with the condition, years before, whilst on holiday in the Canary Islands, and knew exactly what her sister was going through. She had known that caring for Peter was out of the question, until the pain had subsided and her sister's energy returned. Even then, giving Melinda's husband shingles, as a carrier, would have complicated Peter's ability to fight the cancer within him. Melinda had needed to be so careful around him.

Melanie was there, with James, her partner, three weeks before Peter's passing; taking them both to Fishguard for a long weekend. A bed and breakfast break that, despite Melinda's husband's deterioration, had been indulged in for all the right reasons. Yes, Peter was in pain, and having to feed him via a tube in his stomach, was difficult at times. He had loved his food and cups of tea, but couldn't enjoy either of them. Everything had to be put into a syringe and injected into his stomach. The chance of choking and fluids entering his windpipe would have killed him, for sure.

The evening of the last day away, now safely back home, had resulted in his tube coming loose, and an urgent drive to A and E to secure his feeding mechanism as quickly as possible; any more than three hours and the hole in his stomach area would have closed up. With a very high heart rate, Peter was kept in overnight to keep a check on him. His deterioration continued from there, resulting in his demise just weeks later. Melinda's sister had visited him in the hospital, finally being there with Melinda and Stephanie at their home for the last few days of Peter's life.

Promises were kept, his instructions and his final wishes. Melinda had then had to, to her best ability, cope alone. She wasn't completely alone though, not if she was completely honest with herself. She had Amanda, Melanie and James (her partner), and her youngest brother and sister-in-law. Trying to be independent had worked most of the time, she had held her guard well. There were times she had failed, becoming a blubbering mess of constant tears, behind closed doors. Nobody had told her how hard life was without your soulmate; she knew now and it wasn't all chocolates and roses, far from it!

Melinda had busied herself on the laptop, dealing with everything holiday related; putting the final touches in place. Ireland wasn't far off, just a week or so away. Currency had needed to be purchased, Euros to be precise. Amanda's return telephone call, requesting Euros for her, as well as Melinda, had held excitement and feelings of euphoria, something well needed at the moment.

She suddenly had a purpose and somewhere to go other than her own home. Ireland was an unknown entity, although Melinda had a pretty picture in her head as to how she envisaged the country. It wouldn't be long now, and she would know if her expectations were indeed correct. The mystery of the Emerald Isle soon to be discovered. Peter would be with her there too, though not in person. His passport was included in her luggage bag as confirmation; a silent partner, but there all the same.

The week had flown by and they were both finally on their way to Ireland, with an initial two hour stop in Carmarthen town. Being a Sunday, a roast beef dinner was consumed before returning to the coach, and forward bound for Enniscorthy, their hotel for the duration of the coach break. Treacy's hotel it was to be, ironic really, Amelia's maiden name was Tracey. Maybe there were descendants of theirs linked to the hotel chain, it was a definite possibility, not out of the equation.

The Turkey and Tinsel break had turned out to be all Amanda and Melinda had expected, and more. Enniscorthy was the olde world shopping town Melinda had hoped for. Small shops full of character with coffee shops depicting their own unique emblem, their individual stamp on the town's history. They both loved it for what it was, with their hotel located across the stone bridge with the river running underneath it. Picture perfect and something that would have been Peter and Melinda's ideal haven to explore.

The hotel was exactly what they would have requested; nothing prim and proper, just friendly staff and standard hotel rooms. The Christmas trees and decorations adorned the whole building, and the bar and lounge area was the comfy night-time experience Melinda had hoped for. Looking like a library at the top of the stairs, it was actually a part of the lounge itself, and appeared very inviting, and was. Irish music playing every evening, and Christmas songs sung to the early festive season guests. So typically Irish, the atmosphere was perfection in itself. A few white wines and pink gins every evening had sealed the break and created the ambience required.

Dublin was a much larger and more modern commercial shopping area, with an array of different shops to visit and purchase presents to take back home. Melinda had expected Dublin to be a much larger place to explore and wasn't disappointed at all. Cafes and food eateries were in abundance, choices of where to and what to eat not restricted, by any means. The trams, buses and taxis evident everywhere, to get you where you wanted to go in the capital of the country.

Waterford was less commercialised, with a multitude of smaller and older buildings around, tiny shops selling Irish memorabilia alongside the bigger chain stores. The famous Waterford crystal was to be the first stop, with the showroom exhibiting beautiful pieces, and some with prices completely out of their budget. Gorgeous lumps of crystal lovingly turned by workers, into perfect masterpieces; no imperfections were allowed.

A visit around the foundry, watching the experienced people lovingly completing their individual Waterford designs, was an eye-opener. So much artistic talent in creating each piece, any imperfections being returned to the kiln and redone again and again until they were happy with the end product. Anything from a rugby ball, a candelabra, to a pair of intricate drinking glasses, the list of objects made were endless. Melinda had purchased a pair of flute glasses for

Stephanie and her husband, Amanda purchasing an ornament for a friend's birthday.

Peter had worked in an aluminium foundry for years, but Melinda had never visited the inside of it itself, in all the time he had been employed there. His job would have been very similar to the Waterford foundry, albeit using the popular metal rather than the Waterford glass. Hard and dedicated work, day after day. Melinda had asked one of the employees working on an intricate piece of crystal, whether he had found the work monotonous, merely out of curiosity. The answer had been "at times", but he had thoroughly luxuriated in finishing his piece of workmanship, admiring the end result with passion.

Peter's finished product was usually commercial items, in the aluminium foundry; fridge freezer feet, one Melinda had promptly recalled. He had at one time, brought back a dozen and more crocodiles which he had painted green and white, painstakingly accurate, in the garage at home, giving them to the children's school fete to sell for monies for their school fund. By the afternoon of the actual fete, they had all sold and they were asking for more. A proud smile had adorned his face then, so happy that his creations had all gone and so quickly! One of them still remains in Melinda's garden, but the paintwork has now tarnished, something she wouldn't attempt to rejuvenate to its former condition. Artistry wasn't something she would even try, to recreate the crocodile Peter had brought to life. She had laughed to herself just thinking about it. Peter's beaming smile was there, pleased with the school's goal, their achievement to date, his hard work, and its success.

Ireland's landscape was mesmerising, at times. Picture postcard perfection, the cameras or mobile phones click-clicking at speed, trying to capture the scenery whilst sat in the coach drinking it all in. Bums sat on seats, becoming firm friends with all there for the five day break. Pleasant companions at the dinner table; refreshing conversation whilst consuming the tasty food each evening. A Christmas day rehearsal at the beginning of December, all so tastefully done.

The barman had become Father Christmas for the evening, dressed up in his red and white finery, befitting Santa Claus exactly. Mulled wine offered as a hot toddy whilst eating the Christmas lunch. Crackers on the dining table and Christmas melodies playing in the background. The hotel's detail to the festive season was precise, no expense spared. Turkey and tinsel at its best!

Melinda had never smoked cigarettes in her lifetime and never would (a fear of fire from a young age, she would have struggled to light a match or flick a lighter), but Amanda had enjoyed the habit. The rear of the hotel had included a smoking area for those who had entertained it; a heated outdoor bench there to keep them warm in the cold winter weather. She had never seen anything like it, and though not a smoker, would sit there with Amanda whilst warming her bum with her and any other residents in the hotel. A definite talking point and a welcome addition for everyone there who had needed it. Posh! Definitely not, but quirky would probably be a good description. A major talking point, and a good one.

The room they had both accommodated had a double and a single bed, plenty of wardrobe space and a television mounted on the wall opposite the beds. The bathroom had looked, on its first inspection, to be more than adequate for their needs. Amanda had first tried out the bath, only having a shower in her own home, a change for her. A shout from the bathroom, more like a yell really, calling for Melinda's help, had had her in stitches. Within a few minutes of entering the hot water bath, she had been sat in an empty one, and the water had disappeared completely. A mention at dinner time was given to one of the receptionists there. Melinda had tried it herself the next day, only to see the same thing happen. It was showers after that, but hadn't ruined the holiday at all. A good memory to recall when needing a laugh or two.

If there was anything to complain about, it would have been the choppy sea on the return ferry from Rosslare to Pembroke Dock. Melinda's head was so fuzzy with the continual rocking of the ferry, something that hadn't occurred on the travelling over to Ireland. The sea had been calm then, no waves at all; walking steadily throughout the entire length of it, hadn't been a problem, not then.

Lying down on one of the sofas and trying to sleep, was all she could do to alleviate the dizziness. Having managed to travel without too much consequence, as a rule, the ferry's motion had let her down badly. A rare occurrence for Melinda and something completely alien to her. A pounding head wasn't good, not at all. Amanda managed it okay, checking out the duty free shop and balancing really well, considering. She had even carried takeaway coffees from the cafe area without spilling a drop. Melinda's attempt at the duty free shop did produce a purchase eventually, once the waves had resolved to slow down. The coffee was declined for fear of bringing the contents up somewhere. An empty stomach was preferred, in the circumstances. A bout of sickness she didn't need. Better to be safe than sorry.

Had the break ticked all the boxes for them both? Absolutely, and Peter would have agreed, wholeheartedly. He would have been singing with the resident band of an evening, or alongside them loudly, singling out the Elvis Presley songs he'd loved, without any doubt. Missing out on Ireland would have been a deep regret for him, but Melinda truly hoped that he was by their side, drinking in all of the beautiful scenery, and listening to the friendly Irish residents, all too eager to please their tourists.

Ireland had now received a tick against Melinda's bucket list, with only a few things remaining left to do. A return journey to Majorca, a place called S'illot and residing at the same hotel; somewhere Peter had wanted to revisit, but hadn't been well enough to travel there. An elephant ride was still there for Melinda, in a country where the ride was mandatory, all completely normal, rather than in a local UK zoo. Would she be able to place a tick against it before her time was up? Who knew, not Melinda, a complete mystery and a hopeful happening in the future, perhaps.

Chapter Twelve

Christmas, the season to be jolly, supposedly, a festive occasion and a reason to put happiness before sorrow. A getting together of family and friends who would normally incur busy lives, unable to meet up and enjoy one another's company during the rest of the year, merely because time wouldn't allow it. Throughout Melinda and Peter's marriage, their time together had become a mishmash of different ways to celebrate the birth of Jesus Christ, the son of God, born to proclaim a message of hope and redemption.

Christmas proclaims a message of love. "For God so loved the world that he gave his one and only son, that whoever believes in him shall not perish but have eternal life." Christmas proclaims a message of singularity. When we see that baby in the manger of Bethlehem, we are looking at the provision God has made for the sins of the world. There's only one way for humanity to be rescued from its dark impending judgement. It is natural for men and women of the world to believe that "all paths lead to heaven". That is thought to be very sophisticated today.

Christmas is a dangerous time. There is a real danger of missing its true meaning, in the midst of the most popular holiday of the year. Most of the men and women of this world are given over, without restraint, to all the merriment of the holiday season. This is the time they hope to seek maximum pleasure, to get all you can out of Christmas. Unfortunately, the joys of Christmas for them last only a short time. The hang-over needs to be endured, the bills have to be paid, the excess weight lost, the discouragement has to be endured.

Christmas is an artificial high that requires a price to be paid. The joys are transient and short-lived. The fun you seek at Christmas is a type or a sign or pointer to the greater joy, infinitely fulfilling and lasting for all eternity, which can be yours when you embrace the Christmas child as your saviour. The school nativity plays in the local church was always loved for the message it had portrayed. Melinda had missed seeing her children being young and contributing to the play that was Jesus Christ, in all its glory.

Stephanie, Melinda's daughter, had portrayed Mary, Jesus's mother, in Wales using the country's native tongue. Her dressing up had replicated the virgin Mary in its entirety, until you looked at her feet. She had refused to wear anything except her white trainers! The singing was beautiful, emotional, and had both Peter and Melinda reaching for their handkerchiefs. Everything I do, I do it for you, the popular song sung by Bryan Adams, sung in Welsh by the nativity cast with Stephanie leading was indeed euphoric, to say the least.

How Melinda had wished her daughter still a young child with childlike ambitions. Grown up children they were now, now teaching their own children the same values of life, values taught by their own parents and their parents before them. Grandparents were there to give in to the little darlings, and they did, very frequently. Who wouldn't? They were there to spoil them and be grown up children themselves, all in the line of duty. A duty both Melinda and Peter had relished.

The innocence of the young, captivating their frolicking and energy in the run up to Christmas Day itself, the excitement whilst hoping Santa Claus had come bearing presents for them. Had the children been good enough over the past year? Probably not, but regardless of their behaviour, who would deprive them of Christmas presents? With Santa's wish list written and attached to the fridge, for parents to look at (well Santa Claus to study really), how could anyone refuse giving into their hopeful wishes.

Melinda had always far exceeded the amount of presents given to Stephanie's two boys, but in all fairness had bought things for them over the twelve months preceding the end of the year. It hadn't all been purchased in the month of December. Peter had never complained about the endless presents the boys' had opened on the twenty-fifth of the month, being a child himself and indulging in opening his own presents, whether it was one present or twenty-one of them.

The youngest grandson had indicated that his daddy would have to let the log burner fizzle out, in order to allow Santa Claus to come down the chimney. Counting the number of sleeps left to the actual day, with such an innocence and so, so adorable. Melinda could have hugged him, or cwtched him, as the Welsh say. Christmas was definitely for the children with the adults taking in the pure excitement and delight of the day. Happy faces were the result of true happiness.

The previous Christmas had had Melinda, Stephanie, Drew and the two boys, along with Drew's parents and niece, holidaying in France; a skiing break due to not wanting to stay at home on Peter's first festive break after his passing. Melinda had never before entertained a skiing extravaganza, knowing full well that being able to ski with her physical disabilities was impossible, no question about it. In the light of the other only option though, Melinda had agreed to the break after being told that she hadn't needed to ski whilst there. Peter would have laughed at the thought of even mentioning such a holiday, Melinda had known for certain. The trip would not have happened, not in a million years.

Christmas day in snowy France was an experience, a good one. With her walking stick and her snow boots on, she hadn't slipped or fallen down once, even though she had expected to. Dressed up in the essential clothes for the weather, she hadn't felt cold at all. The numerous hot toddies had warmed the cockles, as Amelia would have said if she was there to talk to. Hot chocolate drinks and mulled wine warmed to the right temperature, created the ambience required on the week long break. Melinda had loved it and would venture there again, something she wouldn't have admitted to without actually experiencing it first-hand.

Peter wasn't there with Melinda, even the youngest grandson had missed him; he had asked for his granddad, but not the granddad that was there sat at the dining table, "the other granddad" he had uttered. So, so sweet, for a four year old then. A small being, trying to understand where Peter, his grandfather had gone, and so wishing his return to balance his normal day to day routine. As he gets older, things will fall into place, but for now it was baffling and bewildering for him.

Melinda had recalled the time when the oldest grandson was his age, not understanding why his grandma had needed to wear a scarf on her now bald head. It hadn't suited him, his grandma was his grandma, no matter what she had looked like. The scarf was pulled from her head instantly, before being thrown in a kitchen cupboard, well out of sight. She had never worn scarves again in the house, only putting them on when going outside. He had been right, with or without hair, Melinda was and always would be his grandma.

With Christmas day now on the horizon again, how time had flown without even realising it. Presents were plentiful, all stored in the top box in her bedroom, but Melinda would always keep buying until Christmas Eve, whether she had needed to purchase anything else or not. A way of trying to promote the mood for the upcoming festive season maybe, but with the Christmas stock outshining all other goodies in the supermarkets, it wasn't hard to continue purchasing other presents, or more Christmas food.

With all the countries in the thick of the coronavirus pandemic, the year 2020 was so much more difficult, and travelling abroad to celebrate the occasion was something not permitted, whether that had been the plan initially, or not. Home in bubbles allowed, Melinda would be spending Christmas day with Stephanie and her family, but without Peter. Eighteen months may have passed since his death, but the grief was still there, and the emptiness without him remaining unchanged.

She recalled the Christmas break a few years back, with them both experimenting by booking a weeks' holiday beginning on Christmas Eve and ending on New Year's Eve. Would they rejoice in being away from home during the popular time of the year? Probably the most important time of all, if Melinda was honest. Unfortunately, it hadn't turned out to be the vacation either of them had expected, sad as it was, but it wasn't all doom and gloom.

A sunny disposition throughout the week, a plus compared to the weather in the UK, but somehow it had appeared so strange and completely out of sync. Not the usual way to celebrate the birth of Jesus Christ, sunshine in December had appeared so alien. Majorca was lovely, but the shops actually open were far and few between. An amusement arcade was open, for all those wishing to lose monies to the establishment; the main issue being they hadn't accepted sterling coins. Peter was flummoxed as to which loose change in Euros could be used. A no go area for certain, as things stood, even though Peter had loved the "OXO" machines back home.

As expected, McDonald's was open, why wouldn't they be? Neither of them were keen on the food there, but as a stop gap it was okay, acceptable they supposed. Ordering from the menu in Spanish was a different matter altogether, and attempting to get the retail staff to understand the foods ordered in English, even more discerning. Trying the hotel's culinary delights, Melinda had paid extra for Christmas day meal, rather than looking around for a restaurant or taverna on the twenty-fifth of the month. The food was awful, not the Christmas roast they were both used to. Needless to say, they hadn't eaten in the hotel after that. All-inclusive residents were sorely disappointed when speaking to them about the food cooked there.

Walking around the resort in the glorious sunshine was unexpected, alien, but appreciated for its difference. Dressed in shorts and t-shirts instead of winter clothing, feeling the rays of the yellow sun above hitting their bodies, and giving them both a warm glow and a suntan; all good in retrospect. No rain clouds or bitterly cold weather, just sun, sun, and more sun. What more could they want? The answer to that was indeed family, their immediate relatives, and spending a few days with their nearest and dearest.

Peter and Melinda had done it, tried it, and got the t-shirt, but they wouldn't be doing it again if they could help it. A Christmas cruise would have been much better, with good food cooked for everyone to taste, and plentiful at that, alongside seasonal entertainment of an evening; tunes they were both familiar with to sing along to, in English rather than Spanish as a first language. Neither had regretted their decision to book the festive break, it had been a learning curve for them, and without at least trying the vacation, their views on it would never be known. Where some had preferred to go away for Christmas, others weren't smitten with the idea. Peter and Melinda would have been included in the latter decision, if ever asked.

Melinda was brought back abruptly to the present by the ring of the landline telephone. It was Stephanie, wanting to know what Melinda had wanted for Christmas, a present from her and Drew. She had wanted, the last three Christmas's ago, a wedding album of their celebration, Stephanie and Drew's, with photographs taken by the photographer they had hired for the day. Of all the days to rain, their wedding day had to fall on it. The luck of the draw they supposed, but photographs were taken regardless.

Melinda had concocted an album herself, with photographs taken by family and friends, the majority capturing really good takes. There were a few of the hired photographers takes that nobody else had caught, and she had requested some of those, unique as they were, as memorable keepsakes. With Peter no longer with Melinda, the need was more pronounced, more urgent, but appeared more out of reach than ever. Stephanie had loved her dad so much, Melinda knew, but getting her to present her mother with the present she so wanted, wasn't happening, more is the pity.

Melinda hadn't asked for the album when questioned, merely due to her daughter's grief at losing her dad. Not wanting to open up wounds hidden, or upset her with the request, Stephanie's mother had remained silent, accepting whatever her daughter had decided to give her to open on Christmas day. The boys' needs were more important than Melinda's, her mind had told her, so much more. Christmas wasn't Christmas without children, and the boys' grandma had concentrated on them, their wishes, and watching their little faces beam with happiness on opening so many presents.

Sixty-three year olds (almost sixty-four) had memories to treasure, rather than material objects. As long as Melinda's mind had remained sane, the good days would never be forgotten; not everyone could say that! Melinda was one of the lucky ones in the world and had an awful lot of glorious memories, of places seen and never forgotten, as well as forty-five years of being with Peter. Nobody could ever take that away from her, nobody. For that, she was oh so grateful.

Chapter Thirteen

With the Christmas frivolities over for yet another year, Melinda had focused on the ensuing month long holiday to Fuerteventura, now only four weeks away. Stephanie hadn't expected her mother to go through with the plans, not alone anyway. Melinda's only sole journeys had been to her mother's in Bristol, when she was alive, and to hers and Peter's friends in Devon. All journeys made by National Express coaches due to her panic attacks when driving on a busy motorway. Dual carriageways were fine, but anything more than two lanes would turn her head into turmoil, a frenzy; overtaking on the fast lanes she couldn't seem to judge and her confidence became depleted.

Melinda had booked the international hotel situated in the airport for the night before, leaving an easy five minute walk to the departure lounge the following morning. As expensive as the upmarket accommodation was, convenience was all important and she had paid the charge begrudgingly. With the National Express coaches sorted and the bus from Bristol bus station to the airport, the onus was on Melinda catching the local bus outside her house to the coach station in Wales, to begin her epic journey. She was pleased with the travel arrangements confirmed, along with the shuttle from the

Spanish airport to the hotel she would be residing. Nothing should go wrong! Melinda wasn't always that lucky.

Not really needing new clothes for the holiday, Melinda couldn't help herself. New underwear was always purchased before a vacation and promptly added to her suitcase, as a matter of course. Summer additions were added to the winter break, knowing the weather forecast would be sunshine, sunshine and yet more sunshine, throughout the month long trip. New clothes had excited Melinda, given an excuse or a reason to spend money on herself without feeling slightly guilty about it. Rainy day funds were safely put by, so Melinda couldn't see any harm in spending a little amount to flit away on things she'd not deemed essential.

The wardrobe space originally occupied with Peter's clothing had now been extended to her own recently purchased additions. Only keeping Peter's Hawaiian shirts, his leather waistcoat, and newly unworn socks for Stephanie's oldest son to use when at his grandma's home, the empty space hadn't taken long to fill. Peter wouldn't have minded, on the contrary, he would have smiled before laughing loudly. Melinda's husband knew her too well, she could never resist a bargain when out shopping.

New clothes would always be worn when both away, items Peter had never seen before. Melinda would shrug her shoulders when he had asked when she'd bought the clothing item, before saying, somewhat sheepishly 'I've had it for ages.' The red colouring of her cheeks would have given the game away, but Peter wouldn't have begrudged her anything, Melinda had known.

He had more than enough clothes himself, and new garments were purchased regularly for Peter, by Melinda.

Whilst well, he'd never complained about receiving new clothes, as a rule, but as his health had deteriorated he had cussed her for buying more. She had though, continued as she always did, not feeling the new items were a waste of money.

Recalling Peter's mother, a woman without a bad bone in her body, a credit to the community, asking her husband, Peter's father, for a specific winter coat; one she had admired in the shop window a month before Christmas. Ernest had bought it for her, only for her to lose her fight against cancer a few weeks later, probably wearing it on less than a dozen occasions. With Melinda being asked to sort her clothes out after her death, she had picked up the coat and asked him what to do with the outdoor wear. His words uttered were similar to it being a complete waste of money, not Melinda's thoughts at all. In her eyes, the garment had symbolised him giving Peter's mother what she had wanted at the time. All good, rather than something useless. She had loved the coat.

Amelia had enjoyed the few days break with Melinda and her younger sister, when being shown where her father had lived with his grandparents, an initially unknown entity until they had traced the family tree to his birthplace, a workhouse in Warwickshire; It was less than three weeks later that Amelia had died, but on no account did either of them deem the journey a waste of effort and money. Melinda and her sister had felt that their mother had woken up her father's image, in an area she had never visited beforehand, not to her knowledge anyway.

Naming an area nearby whilst there, her recollections as a young child had re-awakened, and a yearly day out spent cherry picking with her extended family, suddenly opened up Amelia's memory from long ago, with a tear or two in her eyes. Better later than never, the hard work in getting Amelia there, via coach, train, and taxi, and in a wheelchair, was well worth the time and expense it had incurred. Wanting to revisit the area again, her wishes, sadly it wasn't meant to be.

With Peter and Melinda's combined ambitions after retirement, to spend month's long vacations in various locations, far and wide, Fuerteventura was just that, one of the locations to explore; one of their future journeys that Melinda's husband wouldn't be a part of, sadly. Once there, at the destination, she knew she would be okay. It was getting there that had been the mountain to climb first, the long journey travelling by coach, bus, plane, and finally the shuttle to the hotel.

Time after time, the jitters would cause Melinda to doubt her abilities in achieving the destination she had chosen, and as the days became nearer the date itself, her confidence had reached a low ebb. The part of her brain pushing her to achieve her goal, or one of them anyway, had won and Melinda was there in her home ready and eager, to do what they both had wanted to do together. Nerves were rattling, but the adventure was about to begin, finally.

Melinda had recalled her holiday with Stephanie, Drew, and the boys, just one month after Peter's passing. Stephanie's employer had asked her to book a vacation rather than returning to the workplace after his "send off". Mentally, the break could help her rather than hinder her career, giving her time away to sort herself out. Melinda's daughter had adored Peter, he had so spoiled her over the years. Melinda had then become the parent trying to discipline both her son and her daughter, and the person disliked for ruling the roost, so to speak. So unfair really, but necessary.

Stephanie's mother hadn't wanted to remain in the house on her own whilst they were abroad, and voicing her concerns to Drew's wife, Melinda's daughter, a phone call to the holiday firm was made; a request to add Melinda to the booked vacation in Majorca. With the departure occurring on the following day, a seat on the plane was confirmed, but she would need to stay in a different hotel to theirs, due to availability and costs. Melinda handed her debit card details to her daughter before returning to her home to pack a suitcase in record timing.

On reaching the hotel that Melinda would be residing for the week, the shuttle had stopped to allow Melinda to get off and pick up her suitcase from the hold. She was the only one getting off there and being dark due to being the early hours of the morning, she pulled her luggage to the receptionist area with trepidation. Peter and Melinda always managed to find their way to their hotel together, and between the two of them discovered the whereabouts of different areas of the complex required.

Melinda was now on her own, a single person having to discover things entirely by herself; she'd not been used to doing things as a sole individual, and hadn't much liked it. The standard accommodation was okay, nothing special but fine for the week. With Stephanie, Drew and the boys just eight minutes away, at the top of the road, their time spent together would be more than ample. She would have her own space, a plus surely? Melinda hadn't convinced herself enough to actually believe it, though.

There were four beds in the large room, accommodation was for just one though, Melinda. Putting her clothes away, making herself a hot drink (she had packed dried milk, sugar, and teabags; a necessity where Peter was concerned) and getting into one of the made up beds, the tears had started to roll. Could she manage to cope without her husband? This was all so unfair. Everything was now so different, so alien to life as it used to be. Melinda hadn't liked it at all and Peter should have been there with her. She had eventually cried herself to sleep, on one of the more expensive breaks she had paid for!

The next morning, a call from Stephanie had put their hotel and Melinda's on the map. She had felt much better knowing exactly where they all were, arranging to meet up for breakfast and coffee. The balcony had looked onto the main road and Melinda could see people walking up and down the shopping area itself. With a cup of tea in her hand, she settled on a chair on the balcony and waited for her family members to turn up. On arrival, they had passed two parks with swings, sliders and roundabouts, and more. Needless to say, the youngest boy had wanted to try the rides out each and every time they had passed it.

With breakfast eaten and finding their bearings between the two hotels, for future reference, the week away was enjoyed as much as either of them possibly could. The circumstances for the vacation was not a normal reason for being there, but it had helped to keep their minds from the sadness of the past few weeks in Wales. The sun shone to everyone's delight, good food eaten, and time spent on the golden sand admiring the stunning views around.

Melinda had placed her beach towel on the sand, and sat on it while Stephanie, Drew and the boys had dipped their toes and bodies into the beautiful blue sea. She was quite happy admiring others around topping up their tans and generally relaxing, speaking amongst themselves. Peter and Melinda had holidayed very near the location a few years back, their first and last taste at spending Christmas abroad. Then, the opened shops were sparse, but today and in July, the summer season, everything was open and people were there in abundance. What a difference a day makes had sprung to mind. It hadn't appeared to be the same place at all, but it was.

As they had packed things up to find a place to eat, Melinda had picked her beach towel up to put in her bag and discovered a large white feather underneath it. Superstition or not, Peter had been there with them, watching the boys' playing in the water without a care in the world. Melinda was convinced. Having cried her eyes out on the flight over, after reading the breakfast menu that included bacon baps (Peter's preference on the plane) Melinda hadn't any need to worry. Peter was there with them. She was adamant on that score.

The boys' had stayed over with her on some evenings, allowing Stephanie and Drew some much needed time on their own. Melinda had loved having them there, it hadn't been an inconvenience at all. The more the merrier, as the saying goes. Melinda's downfall was actually getting into the hotel accommodation itself. The key didn't appear to work the majority of the time, she just couldn't open the door. A change of key hadn't helped either.

On one occasion, Melinda had managed to catch the next door resident to help with the lock, explaining in English to someone speaking a completely foreign language. Two other occasions, a visit from the receptionist opening the door without any problem at all, and with Drew helping at times and the odd moment when she actually managed the lock herself, Melinda's arthritis in her hands had really let her down badly. How she had cussed Peter under her breath, for not being there in person. Melinda had made herself look so stupid, helpless, and a complete and utter fool.

Stephanie and Drew had enjoyed a late night on one of the evenings. With the boys' in her care, a visit to one of the karaoke bars and partaking in a few cocktails, Stephanie had handed the host a piece of paper with her name and a song written down on it that she had wanted to sing. Not unusual for her at all, Peter and his daughter sung well together, as well as a single performer. Melinda, being tone deaf, applauded along with others there when they did perform.

On taking the boys' back to the hotel the following morning, Melinda's daughter had spoken about their evening. There had been a singer on the stage prior to Stephanie's solo performance, a male contender with a good voice, ideal for a karaoke night out. As the words to the song appeared on the screen, the song made famous by the unforgettable Elvis Presley, Stephanie had suddenly felt the goosebumps on her arms. The song In the Ghetto was one frequently sung by her dad, and one Peter had recorded in the Sun Studio in Memphis, Tennessee, when holidaying in the USA.

How special Peter had felt, sat in the same studio of his all-time hero of rock and roll, recording one of Elvis Presley's hits, and walking out with a CD recorded in such a special place. The Sun Studio was opened by rock and roll pioneer Sam Phillips in 1950. It was originally called Memphis Recording Service, sharing the same building with the Sun Records label business. How proud Peter had been, on singing as well as visiting the building that had brought Elvis Presley into the limelight, highlighting his future career. A prominent figure nobody would ever forget.

Having listened to the male vocalist before comparing him to Peter's rendition of the popular song, Stephanie had envisaged her dad there, in full view of everyone else; joining in the karaoke session. Stephanie had sung her song afterwards, but knowing that her dad would have, without a doubt in her mind, sung before her and the identical song the male person had, had somehow spooked Stephanie. Peter had been there, Melinda was more than convinced. The signs were there, definitely. Not a shadow of a doubt.

Coming back to today, and reality, Melinda's suitcase and hand luggage were evident in the living room, ready for her journey beginning after a night's sleep; well maybe a few hours at least. Would Peter be there on her voyage? Her solo trip into going it alone. Melinda had so hoped he would show some evidence of being there with her; anything significant would do, something that would link him positively wherever Peter's wife was.

As she got into bed that evening, her mind had overflowed with this, that, and the other.

Everyone, well almost everyone, had thought she was mad. Perhaps she was, but without trying she would never know. Not being averse to asking questions, speaking to strangers, or relaxing alone, Melinda would soon know if she had indeed made the right decision.

Chapter Fourteen

Melinda stood outside her house waiting for the bus to take her to Swansea bus and coach station, the first leg of her solo voyage to Fuerteventura. Being semi-rural, there were only two buses into the centre of Swansea, and two returning back to her area. She couldn't miss the connection, all the commuting put in place had relied upon it. Being outside her house, she hadn't far to walk to the bus stop, so no excuses needed for missing it.

A couple opposite, well known neighbours, were waiting with her; their usual day for visiting Swansea and meeting up with relatives. As the bus stopped, not the usual one, the driver announced that there weren't any seats vacant due to the original bus having mechanical issues. The replacement vehicle was only a sixteen seater, and all seats were now filled. Melinda's start to her month long vacation had hit a hitch already, she was dumbfounded.

Thankfully, Melinda's neighbours had their own vehicle, but preferred to take the free bus into town. With no other option for them, or Melinda, they kindly drove her to the park and ride, and she had arrived in plenty of time for the first coach of two, heading for Bristol. Phew! Breathing a sigh of relief, Melinda had thanked them, and walked to the coach park to board the coach heading for Cardiff. Another coach from Cardiff to Bristol bus station, then finally the bus to the airport and the international hotel for the night.

Thinking how Peter would have coped with Melinda's ensuing travel programme, she knew that he wouldn't have even entertained it. Buses were rarely her husband's mode of transport. They had caught a few buses when abroad, somewhat reluctantly on Peter's part, but otherwise it would be using the car or remaining at their chosen resort. Melinda had recalled their four day holiday in Venice, a wonderful experience. They had both loved it. Getting used to travelling by water-bus had initially caused Peter to huff and puff, struggling to understand the system on the waterway.

Melinda had asked a few locals what had needed to be done and followed their advice; it had been pretty straightforward really. It was similar to getting on a bus, but on the water, all simple enough. They got on and off at particular stops, picking out areas that they had wanted to explore. St Mark's Square was their first destination and the fabulous church, Saint Mark's Basilica. They had spent hours there, the camera clicking at speed, so much history there to see.

Rialto Bridge and the Bridge of Sighs, two of the finest worth investigating. The Bridge of Sighs, an enclosed bridge made of white limestone, has windows with stone bars, and passes over the Rio di Palazzo, and connects the New Prison to the interrogation rooms in the Doge's Palace. The Rialto Bridge is the oldest of the bridges spanning the Grand Canal in Venice, Italy. It has been rebuilt several times since its first construction as a pontoon bridge in 1173, and is now a significant tourist attraction in the city.

Melinda and Peter had stopped outside the Rialto Bridge, and like many others on the water-bus, had got off to take photographs close up. Climbing the steps and walking across the bridge itself was both historical and modern combined, a good experience. With small shops and food to takeaway on either side of the construction, somehow it was something Melinda hadn't expected, she'd not known why. She had purchased several Venetian masks for presents back home, and a glass necklace she had liked at the time. Nothing expensive, but different, and a piece of costume jewellery she could add to her collection. How often she would wear it was debatable, but what the heck, Melinda was on holiday.

They had both boarded a water-bus after the Rialto Bridge, heading down the canal towards St Mark's Square for a second visit, or so Peter had thought at the time. Melinda wasn't sure that they were on the correct water-bus for the journey, but hadn't argued as Peter had sat down on one of the seats. As they set off, she still wasn't convinced, the seats were facing the wrong way as far as she could tell. The bus had travelled a short way, before turning around and stopping at the exact spot they had got on. They had both egg on their faces. Ooops!

Melinda hadn't trusted her husband after that. It was a laughable experience as they had recalled their journey, but back then, having to retrace their steps and board the right water-bus, had Peter's wife taking more attention to detail. The mini-break was everything Melinda had expected; a historical city, beautifully kept, with all vehicles water based. A gondola ride hadn't been taken on the famous Grand Canal, but all that was done in the four days there, was something neither of them would ever forget.

Thoughts of Amelia had sprung to mind just then; she had shown Melinda a photograph of Venice, one given to her by her carer when mentioning Melinda's booked vacation. Her innocence at not having travelled far in her life and the words directed at her eldest daughter.

'Did you know the city is covered in water?' Amelia had asked very seriously.

Melinda couldn't keep a straight face. Walking to the kitchen area of her one bedroomed flat and putting the kettle on for a cup of tea, she had tried to keep her giggling from her. It wasn't her mother's fault, her knowledge of other countries hadn't been brilliant, but Melinda couldn't contain her composure and headed for the bathroom to let out her laugh, out of earshot of her mother. Bless her!

Peter had never been keen on Italian food, but he had managed okay and hadn't starved. The hotel they had stayed in had Peter tasting their hors d'oeuvres, appetisers or starters at the bar of an evening. Giving the thumbs up or thumbs down, he had relished in being chief taster every evening whilst there. A telephone call on Melinda's mobile, asking her to pick up her grandson from school as he wasn't well, had them both spellbound and smiling. They'd not known that his grandparents were in Venice.

Venice, Rome, and Pisa, were places in Italy they had experienced and had felt exhilarated at being able to see with their own eyes. The Trevi Fountain had received the mandatory coin or coins, the superstition and the myth behind it. If you throw one coin: you will return to Rome. If you throw two coins: you will fall in love with an attractive Italian. If you throw three coins: you will marry the person that you met. The coin or coins should be thrown with your right hand over your left shoulder. Whether truth or baloney, since 2007 the monies recovered from the fountain has been used to support good causes. Regardless of the coins, the Trevi Fountain is the most beautiful fountain in the world, one Peter and Melinda had been privileged to have seen first-hand, and thrown a single coin into it. Would they revisit Rome again? Who knew?

Likewise, the Spanish Steps, a set of steps in Rome, climbing a steep slope between the Piazza di Spagna at the base and Piazza Trinita dei Monti, dominated by the Trinita dei Monti church at the top. The 135 steps, in the middle of the city's shopping district has a ruling that no food is to be eaten on them. A popular place to sit and relax, transfixed with the area around it, Melinda and Peter were gratified in just sitting there for a while.

Pisa and the famous leaning tower. The freestanding bell tower of the cathedral of the Italian city of Pisa, known worldwide for its nearly four-degree lean, the result of an unstable foundation. They had both seen it with their own eyes, the definite listing of the building, and watching tourists climbing it. Florence, capital of Italy's Tuscany region, the home to many masterpieces of Renaissance art and architecture. Its beauty, artistic charm and centuries of history was out of this world, but far too busy for their liking. By far, the area neither of them wanted to revisit, purely because of the human traffic walking in, around, and through it.

Italy, as a country was worthy of its tourists, a beautiful and elegant area of the globe that Melinda had been so glad to have explored. With her solo journey to Fuerteventura on the immediate horizon, she'd needed to have her wits about her. The Canary Islands hadn't the historical architecture of Italy, she knew, but having seen so much of Italy in the past, Fuerteventura was now her goal, to capture it and discover its glory whilst tanning her body in the winter sunshine. All good in her eyes.

It had been a long journey getting to her destination, and having to be at the departures at six o'clock in the morning, Melinda hadn't slept at the hotel. It was crucial that she was there in plenty of time, and it had played on her mind resulting in no sleep at all. At five o'clock in the morning, Melinda was eating breakfast and drinking tea, something unheard of for her; not usually eating breakfast and definitely not at that time of the day. She would be shattered by the time she had got to her location, for sure.

Melinda had purposely booked an early flight, not wanting to arrive in Fuerteventura in the early hours of the morning, in complete darkness. Her holiday in Majorca earlier had taught her a lesson there, especially being a solo traveller. An afternoon arrival had made more sense. Having an idea of her location before the night drew in, would make a difference and hopefully install a few landmarks in her brain. Nothing was guaranteed though, not where Melinda was concerned.

Having disembarked from the plane and collected her luggage from the baggage carousel, the next stage was to find the shuttle bus to her hotel. Strange, but this was the part of Melinda's journey she was most concerned about. Dreading not finding the shuttle bus or getting on the wrong one, her panicking was real. As things turned out, the shuttle wasn't difficult to find, and three other holidaymakers were already sat down, so Melinda had checked with them regarding where the bus was stopping. All good so far, a sigh was released as she settled herself in one of the seats.

On reaching her hotel, the only one getting off the bus, pulling her suitcase to the reception area wasn't difficult. The weather was sunny and hot, a good start, and a key to the bungalow given to her with directions around the complex. It had sounded simple enough, but as was normal for Melinda and Peter, wasn't quite so straightforward. Peter wasn't with her, so no blame could be put on her husband this time.

If Melinda had walked once around the area of the complex where the bungalows were, then she had probably did it three or four times before espying the number that she was looking for. Pulling her suitcase around with her was hard going, Melinda's laptop in her hand luggage became heavier and heavier as she walked the vicinity where she would be staying for the next twenty-eight days. As she put the key in the door of her holiday home, taking the weight off her feet and almost collapsing on the sofa, a huge sigh was exhaled from her body. Melinda had managed to travel from Wales to Fuerteventura, and apart from her neighbours help at the beginning of her journey, she had got there by her own steam. 'Eureka,' she had cried out. 'Eureka!'

Checking out the bungalow, or one-bedroomed apartment as it was, Melinda was pleasantly surprised with the accommodation. Nothing fancy, she wouldn't have wanted posh, the lounge area with a dining table and chairs and a refrigerator for keeping drinks cool; a kettle and cups and saucers for warm beverages. A decent sized television, showing English programmes as well as Spanish trivia. Melinda would still be able to watch the soaps whilst there, all good on the western front. A smile erupted at last, the worry lines disappearing suddenly, before she had even ventured up the stairs to the first floor of the building.

The bathroom was as all bathrooms were, a wash basin, WC, and a good sized shower. Melinda had hoped for a bath with a shower over it, but, disappointed as she was, the room was totally adequate for her requirements. She couldn't complain. The bedroom had twin beds, a decent sized wardrobe, chest of drawers and bedside cabinets. With patio doors leading onto a balcony, complete with furniture, a clothes airer, and a decent view which became a suntrap in the hot weather, who could argue about anything? All appeared good on Melinda's first impression, any roads.

Being an all-inclusive complex, a drink and snack was something Melinda could do with after putting her clothes away tidily. Her medication for the month had found a drawer in one of the bedside cabinets, and toiletries safely deposited on shelves in the bathroom. It had been time to check out the complex and find the restaurant or cafeteria, in search for food and refreshments. As Melinda bypassed the large pool area, noticing a hairdresser, a gym, a supermarket, a souvenir shop, and a board indicating the hotel's entertainment for the coming week, an arrow pointing to the restaurant pushed her towards the eatery.

As she entered the building, furnished with numerous tables and chairs, some accommodating two people and others a family of four or more, the food area being central to the whole building. Access to the self-service cuisine was easy enough, so Melinda picked up a plate and began putting appetising pieces of food onto it. Finding a table to sit on, she placed her choice of meals available on the table, found a glass and a selection of refreshments including white wine and Sangria.

Sangria had won, she was on holiday after all. Tucking into her food, Melinda had looked forward to the many days and evenings that she would savour the cuisine of the hotel. The first impression was bordering on excellent, only time would tell if it remained that way.

Chapter Fifteen

The weather was still warm when Melinda had finished eating her meal, so getting a feel of the complex itself had sounded good. Taking in the other amenities that she had missed whilst looking for the restaurant, the complex itself was larger than she had initially envisaged. Espying the tennis court as she wandered about leisurely, a definite no to taking part there; it was nice to know where it was. Someone else might be looking for it!

The pool itself was large in size, surrounded by sun loungers aplenty. No-one appeared to be in the water, hinting that it wasn't a heated pool, and more than likely cold. A pool bar was there for refreshments, both hot and cold, the bar staff there ready and willing to oblige its residents for whatever length of time they were there. With several tables and chairs around it, Melinda had decided to partake in another sangria and sit there for a while. Her eyes hovered from one side of the pool to the other, checking out the buildings around whilst following the map of the complex given to her by the receptionist.

According to the map, a Jacuzzi was somewhere around, costing 5 Euros for an hour's visit. Slots had required to be booked beforehand at the reception area, along with the fee applicable; the key to the Jacuzzi was kept there, too. Melinda had needed to check that out, she had so appreciated a spell in the hot tub with the everlasting foaming bubbles. It was very therapeutic, and eased the pain in her stomach (where she had her operation years before) whilst relaxing completely. Her brain shutting down whilst bathing in it. Heaven itself.

There was no urgency, but Melinda had needed to know where things were, and not merely out of curiosity. Her head wouldn't rest without acquiring all the details needed, Melinda's make-up since a child. Pondering over things until she'd answered her own questions satisfactorily, a more than possible reason her sleep pattern was consistently all over the place back home.

The Gym area was passed by at first before stopping and walking through the door and noticing the word Jacuzzi, written quite plainly on one of the doors inside the building. Hooray, she had found it. Melinda's smile had shown excitement. With no bath in her bungalow, a few visits to the Jacuzzi whilst there, was a more than probable date, even if it was to be on her own.

Still studying the map, the entertainment lounge and bar was found. Nothing special, if Melinda was honest. A large bar area with scattered tables and chairs inside and outside the premises. Not being a big drinker, she did enjoy the occasional alcoholic shot, and it was indeed occasional. Latte's and hot chocolates usually won over the alcoholic choice when home in the UK. Bearing in mind that Melinda's all-inclusive vacation had included all refreshments, whether alcoholic or not, maybe trying a few hot and cold toddies would pass her lips during her stay there. It wouldn't hurt to sample a few of their cocktails, surely.

A browse around the souvenir shop on the complex had required the mandatory stroll. Not being a large building, but selling unique goods, mostly from local creative artists. Her mind had noted some pieces of bric-a-brac and jewellery, before leaving the shop knowing there had been plenty of time to purchase items there.

Melinda had found the children's play area, and the smaller pool area that had been separated from the larger one. For perfect relaxation and seclusion, the smaller of the two would have been preferable. Melinda hadn't booked the break to hide herself away, more to the contrary. She wanted to enjoy the holiday for what the complex was, and that wasn't to remain in solitude. There must be some holidaymakers there that had copied Melinda's purpose for being there alone, for whatever reason. She was about to find out. Fuerteventura was about to be explored by her and her husband; Peter had to be there watching over her, hadn't he?

The small garden in front of Melinda's home whilst there, an earthed area with a tree and flowers blooming in the border, was hers and hers alone for the duration. There was enough room to put a chair on the small patio area, and read, write, and relax, her choices. Shielded from the sun, a perfect place to sit and think. About what, Melinda had asked herself? Anything, everything, or nothing at all; Melinda's moments for doing whatever she had wanted to do. Something pretty scarce while she was caring for her sick husband. How Melinda had so wanted Peter there with her. Absence makes the heart grow fonder, how true that was in the present time, now and forever.

The hairdresser's prices were noted in her mind, maybe a future appointment. Also engaging in massages and spa treatment, not really Melinda's cup of tea, but never say never. Leaving the outside of the complex to pursue another day, Melinda had made herself a cuppa in her bungalow, sat on the sofa and suddenly, without warning had fallen asleep. The last two days had included a lot of commuting, coaches, buses, and planes. Lack of sleep had suddenly affected her alert mind, now that she had finally reached the place of her dreams; she had hoped it was, anyway.

On waking up, in the late afternoon, so unusual for her, the time on her watch had indicated that evening meals would be open to residents in the restaurant. Melinda hadn't changed her clothes, but had washed her face and hands before brushing her hair. Trying to lock the door as she had picked up her small handbag, somehow it wouldn't lock at all. Her hands weren't conforming again it had seemed. After numerous attempts, a visit to see the receptionist was her first stop. Explaining the problem at the reception area, she was told to return to her bungalow and wait for a maintenance person. She had mentioned a name, a male Christian name, but in today's world a Christian name wasn't always obvious as to the gender of the person. Melinda couldn't presume, and hadn't.

Luckily, Melinda hadn't waited long. The man had taken her keys and rather than lifting the handle before placing the key into the lock, he had pushed the handle down. The door was locked, and she had blushed, red faced at the simplicity of his movement. A naive teenager she wasn't but had recalled her younger years, and the embarrassed moments of the past, and there were several of them, sadly.

There had been another problem that Melinda had noticed whilst in the bungalow and she had explained the issue to the man stood in front of her. The bathroom was a bright and airy room during the daytime. Melinda couldn't find a light switch to use when the night had set in and had relied on the light at the top of the stairs to see. Walking up the staircase, following the maintenance technician, he had put his hand inside the bathroom door and flicked a switch, a switch that Melinda had thought belonged to the shaver connection. She had done it again, the red face had reappeared.

As Melinda had taken her eyes from the bathroom, she had glanced into the bedroom. The door was open, no requirements to close it with her being the only person inhabiting the place anyway. On one of the beds, a black and white cat had made itself at home, curled up in a comfy ball. The cat had woken up and ran down the stairs before exiting the main patio door, the front of the bungalow. There were no words, just pure astonishment. Asking how the cat had got in, to the maintenance technician, completely aghast, he had shrugged his shoulders before leaving Melinda in the bungalow.

Walking back to the restaurant, the door now firmly locked, she helped herself to food on the evening's menu. A refreshing orange juice was poured and Melinda found a table for two to sit down. There were a lot of people there feeding their ever hungry stomachs, after sunning themselves around the pool most of the day, or on the balconies where many were definite heat traps. The food was good, plenty of choice; waiters refreshing the empty containers in quick succession, and topping up the salad bar when required. Going hungry was never going to happen, not with the variations and amount of culinary delights available.

Melinda was still puzzling over how the cat had managed to park herself on the spare bed in her bedroom, whilst she tucked into her food. A lightbulb moment suddenly occurred, realising that whilst asleep in the afternoon, the door had been ajar to let the air in. The cat must have climbed the stairs and made itself comfy then. Having had her last cat, Cleo, for twenty years, Melinda wasn't averse to the feline creatures at all. Maybe she had found a friend to keep her company for the duration of her holiday!

Melinda's laptop was placed on the small table at the side of the sofa. There was a small notepad that she had included in her luggage, there to take notes when inspiration had injected her brain. After writing only three chapters of a novel in over a year, Melinda had hoped to resurrect them from the cobwebs and try to complete the writing in the month in the sunshine.

She hadn't been lazy or anything like that, having Peter to nurse and look after, the hours just didn't allow her any free time to be creative and pick up the laptop to write. If Melinda could fill a few pages, or a few chapters, then at least she could say she'd tried. As if fate had actually sent her to a sunny coastal area, the novel had begun with a shy young man travelling abroad for a month without his extroverted sister, who had sadly passed away just weeks earlier.

Had she picked the best spot to bring out her creative instincts, to turn visions into ideas, and words transported to her partly written novel? The complex itself could produce a hotel whereabouts for the young man in question, but Melinda had needed to venture out into the area around it, and create an illusive presence in his character; something to grip a storyline and keep readers alive, wanting to read more. Could Melinda do that? Only time would tell.

Breakfast was served in the restaurant between 8.30am and 10.30am, so she got up early the following morning to see what was on the menu. A short walk outside afterwards, she had decided. The novel wouldn't get written without it, and Melinda had wanted to venture out, any roads. If she had lost her way, then she had all day to retrace her steps and find her hotel again; time was immaterial when on holiday. Peter had always said that and it was totally true, no arguments there.

The difference being that Melinda was there for four whole weeks to really get to grips with her storyline, as well as there to take in the beauty of the coastal area, and devour the holiday itself. There were no right or wrong answers as to what Melinda did in the days and evenings there; no-one to judge her, tell her off, or analyse her for that matter. She was her own person, to do whatever she wanted to do, whenever she wanted to do it.

Staying in bed all day would have been her prerogative, if that had been her choice, but Melinda's mind had wanted to explore, and the sooner the better. The breakfast menu was good, everything anyone could want early in the morning. Egg, bacon, sausages, baked beans, tomatoes; toast and yoghurt, and refreshing juices to wake your senses up in preparation for the day ahead.

Walking out of the reception area, picking up several leaflets to read on her travels, Melinda headed for the coast, something she could see vividly from her balcony. It couldn't be that far away, could it? Time would tell as she continued walking the pavement opposite the hotel. Passing an Irish bar, a mini-market, and another interesting bar named The Crazy

Goat, all situated right next to one another. On her own, Melinda wouldn't have entered the bars, or so her brain had told her.

Maybe her confidence would increase enough to partake in a drink or two on her own later, she could hope anyway.

As she continued walking down the path towards the sea, another chain of buildings emerged in front of her. All eateries; an Indian restaurant, a Mexican restaurant, a Chinese restaurant and a restaurant seemingly selling English based food by the menu outside. Sunday roast was written on one of the boards, a reasonable cost, and something she had decided to try at least once whilst there.

Melinda continued past the rank of eateries, crossing the road to a pathway leading to the blue sea beyond. Another road crossed and Melinda was now sitting on a rock admiring the glorious views in front of her, the crystal blue sea and beyond. The silence around was idyllic, a chance to merely sit and ponder. Thinking without any restrictions, about whatever had taken her fancy. Watching the birds, gulls mostly, flying in the air at their own pace; a few fisherman settled on rocks at the base of the cliff edge, their rods eager to catch something on the end of it, a fish or two.

Glancing around, if she had headed right, a stone built pathway following the coast appeared to head into a town, an area with several buildings where roofs were visible from where she had sat, lots of them. People were walking up and down the path, stopping at concrete benches for well needed breathers, she had guessed. To the left, apart from residential buildings, the area was barren, sand afoot for a long stretch before any type of building was visible.

A few photo shots were taken on her phone before heading back to the hotel. She would venture further in a day or so, but for now Melinda was happy enough with her surroundings seen so far. Were they inspirational for her novel, not as yet, but her mind had held her visions inside. They weren't lost and could take up a paragraph or two, or not, as the case may be. A refreshment was required, the sun heating up fast. Dehydration wasn't something Melinda had wished upon herself and the large varieties of liquid refreshments were fully paid in the hotel. It was a no brainer.

Chapter Sixteen

A few refreshing soft drinks sat around the pool bar, before finding an empty sun lounger nearby and planting her body upon it, was all good for the soul. Included in her beach bag was a Mills and Boon novel, a short read that always had a happy ending, usually romantically inclined. Melinda wasn't averse to longer novels, but holiday mode was usually less heavier books with easier and more obvious reads. Carrying a few of them in her luggage, she had wanted to read them whilst there, rather than having to take them back home with her again.

There was a gentle breeze around the pool now, the cloud almost concealing the yellow sun in the sky above. Bodies were moving and returning to their holiday accommodation, after melting themselves in the hot sun most of the day. Melinda remained reading for an hour, maybe a tad longer; she hadn't looked at her watch before copying them and going back to her bungalow. A cup of tea before showering and changing into evening clothes, nothing special, but not something as revealing as swimwear or shorts and t-shirt. The weather wasn't cold, but as the evening wore on, a cardigan or summer coat was required if partaking in a drink or two after the evening meal.

As Melinda sat on the sofa, gazing at the English programmes on the television, a meow, meow was heard at the patio door. The doors had been shut firmly because of her showering and changing her clothes upstairs. Drawing the curtain back to investigate, the black and white moggy from the previous evening was sat there, urgently waiting to come inside. Melinda partly opened it, allowing the pretty feline to enter. She (it was too pretty to be a he) watched closely, curious as to what or where she would go.

The cat had been fed and watered, not in need of either food or drink. Her coat was smooth and glossy, proof that she was well looked after. No collar though, not that having one had any relevance, not really. Watching her climb the stairs and settle herself on the spare bed, Melinda had left her there. The soaps were on, something Melinda followed when home alone, and although the television had at intervals, become blank, she hadn't lost any parts of the programme itself or missed any of the storyline. Perhaps a trip to the reception area again if it continued to play up.

As time elapsed, evening meal at the restaurant was open to its residents, and Melinda was hungry. Her tummy was rumbling, she'd not eaten much all day. Breakfast had sufficed throughout the day, and lunchtime munching wasn't required. In her own time, she would probably manage three meals a day, just because they were available. Her metabolism required getting used to more food digested on a regular basis. Melinda was sure her body would adjust to the changes quite easily, given time.

Evening meal was as good as the previous evening. A change in culinary delights, but all seeming completely edible and looking delightful. A salad first, with the garlic dressing covering the lettuce, cucumber, and tomatoes. Cold meats and cheese were there to add to the meal. The dressing itself was irresistible, so yummy. Melinda used the garlic dressing every time she had chosen a healthy salad on the menu from then on. Refreshing orange juice and ice cream as a dessert, various flavourings, she was happy enough.

Walking from the restaurant to the lounge area minutes away, a sangria at the bar was decided and poured into a glass, rather than in a disposable cup. The seats inside the lounge area were full, no spare seats or tables to be found. Melinda wasn't used to sitting at the bar, especially as a lone traveller. Finding a seat outside, she drank her sangria slowly, people watching as her mother used to do. Connecting couples together as well as families, she hadn't noticed any lone travellers there.

In the restaurant, the holidaymakers travelling alone were more obvious. Sitting on a table for two, on their own, a few gentlemen stood out, as did one lady. Did she want to be on her own though, Melinda had asked herself? Would approaching her and conversing with the lady in question be the correct approach? She didn't want to intrude, if being alone on holiday was her preferred vacation.

Melinda was very new to all of this and making a laughing stock of herself wasn't something she had wanted to do. If, on the other hand, Melinda was approached by ladies realising that she was travelling without a companion, then the matter would be completely different. She hadn't got the hang of things just yet, and after forty-five years with Peter it had been no wonder. There was no way she would have approached the gentlemen on their own. Melinda wasn't after another relationship, now or in the future. Both Melinda and Peter were there, in her head. Only Melinda was visible though.

Talking, Melinda had loved to talk. Amanda would confirm that, without a doubt. At times, Melinda's friend couldn't get a word in edgeways. Circumstances were different in Fuerteventura, with people being where they were for purposes some would happily discuss, whilst others preferred to remain silent and completely hidden away. Each and every one of us having choices made by ourselves personally, for whatever reason, whether right or wrong, no arguments there.

Recalling a weeks' holiday in Portugal years' back. Meeting an aged gentleman and his forty year old daughter, a lady having physical and learning disabilities. Conversation one evening with the gentleman, whilst sitting next to them in the entertainment lounge, was exhilarating and also so knowledgeable. Taking his daughter to Portugal on his own had been due to his wife passing away a year earlier. He had adored his wife, missing her terribly. His daughter, having Down's syndrome, required a lot of care; Peter had admired his determination to carry on with life, and his coping so admirably with the daughter he loved, when not exactly a spring chicken himself.

It had taken a lot of coaxing for him to talk about his late wife, but a few days after meeting him, he did just that. Discussing his life back in the UK, he opened up to his heartache at losing her. She had nursed him through a triple heart operation, lovingly doing what was required to bring him back to the man she had married. Sadly, she was diagnosed with a brain tumour shortly afterwards, passing away way before her time and leaving him to bring up their daughter alone.

It had been his second marriage, the first one dissolved amicably between the two of them. There were children from his first relationship, all still in contact with him and his youngest daughter. Feeling that they had their own lives to live, he hadn't asked for help in bringing up their half-sister, although there were occasions when his oldest daughter did take her out for a day or two, giving him some much needed space. His dedication to her was second to none, he so loved the daughter conceived with his late wife, disabilities or not.

Both Melinda and Peter had taken them under their wings, escorting them to the old part of the town via the local noddy train. A vehicle resembling an adult's toy train set with several compartments to sit and enjoy the ride around the streets of the vicinity. Only four stops away, the old town was a place worth seeing; a picture postcard of days gone by. With a fountain located in the centre of the square and quaint shops and eateries covering the outside of it, it represented Portugal at its best. A leisurely stroll around the market stalls, a drink in one of the eateries listening to the music played by the resident musician, playing pan pipes so, so beautifully. Melinda could have remained there for hours; a perfect afternoon for the four of them, one to remember for the best of reasons.

Melinda and Peter had felt for him and his daughter. After getting her husband well after a heart operation, she'd lost her own life to something they couldn't fix, leaving him heartbroken. Pretty similar to what had occurred between Peter and Melinda, she had realised. Peter was there to get Melinda through breast cancer, as Peter was diagnosed with terminal lung cancer. How cruel life was! Peter hadn't wanted to lose Melinda, and hadn't. It was Melinda who had lost Peter, all seemed so unfair and unexpected, whilst Melinda was recovering herself.

Back into today's world, Melinda had noticed that karaoke night was the evening's entertainment. She had decided to stay and listen to the resident singers, good or bad, reminiscing Peter's love of amateur singing. Rolling out the Elvis Presley songs with the microphone to his lips, Melinda's husband's claim to fame. Indulging in his guilty pleasure on holiday. She was so going to miss that. The host, a young Spanish girl, had tried her best to arouse singers to the stage, but in all honesty, the singers were far and few between. Resorting to young children being given the microphone, the entertainment wasn't that good. The angelic voices singing nursery rhymes and the like, was sweet, very sweet, but Peter wasn't there and Melinda hadn't wanted to stay too long. Memories, distant as they were, became emotional; she was near to tears.

Deciding to call it a day, Melinda returned to her bungalow. A cup of tea taken to her bedroom along with her partly read novel, an early night was called for. The black and white cat was still there, curled up on the spare bed, happily sleeping. Melinda had opened the patio door in her bedroom a little, enough for her to escape if she'd wanted to go out. She hadn't though, and on Melinda getting inside the covers, the docile moggy had jumped onto the bed she was in, curling up at the bottom of it. She had found a companion, a four legged one!

Nothing had been done to her writing, not as yet anyway. There was plenty of time, and if at the end of the holiday nothing had been added to her chapters written so far, it wasn't the end of the world. The notebook and pen remained in her beach bag, along with a large beach towel, ready for any inspirational moments that might occur. That hadn't been forthcoming as yet, but Melinda was sure that somewhere along the line her pen would write something on the notebook, and Melinda's novel would at least increase in chapters, if not fully completed or to her satisfaction.

Turning the bedside lamp off and closing the pages of the novel, Melinda had tried to sleep, something she struggled to do even back home. With the stress relieved and Melinda in holiday mode, surely sleep would come easier! She could only hope for a peaceful night, as Melinda's companion changed her position and decided to park herself higher up the bed, as Melinda curled her body into a ball, not dissimilar to the friendly moggy's position.

There was no rush to get up the next morning. Breakfast could be missed. An hour after breakfast was finished, the restaurant opened up again for snacks; a hot dog, beefburger and onions, both with the optional bread roll or bap. Non-alcoholic beverages, including tea and coffee. Melinda wasn't going to starve, far from it.

Unfortunately, the choice of Melinda's time to get out of bed wasn't hers. The cat jumping off her bed and meowing loudly to her, had woken her up. Obviously wanting to go out, but not happy at exiting via the patio doors in the bedroom, she had wanted to leave via the door downstairs. Melinda had let her out, putting the kettle on for a cup of tea and settling on the sofa. A quick shower afterwards before dressing in shorts and t-shirt, and it was time for the restaurant to open for breakfast. Replacing her novel in the beach bag, she walked slowly taking in areas of the complex she had missed along the way. There was always something else to see, something she hadn't noticed before.

It was cloudy, the sun not wanting to play just yet. As Melinda had entered the restaurant, busier than the day before, a seat was found and cereal, a cup of tea, and toast eaten and drank. A second cup of tea, before espying fresh fruit at the bottom of the food tables. Picking up an orange, Melinda peeled and ate it in her own time. Deciding to venture further along the path by the coast, heading for the built up area in view, and with the weather cloudy at present, it had made complete sense to Melinda.

Ensuring she had put her purse in her beach bag, she walked out of the complex well prepared for a day investigating the area around, and further afield. Getting lost was always par for the course where Peter and Melinda were concerned. James, Melanie's partner, was a dab hand at it too, getting lost that was. Numerous occasions were remembered, merely due to taking the wrong direction, by foot or by car. It was always a conversation where laughing was compulsory, remembering times filled with hysteria, after the event. At the time, no-one was laughing.

Recalling Melinda's son's wedding in Greece, Rhodes to be exact. Whilst Peter, Melinda, Stephanie and her young son then, Melinda's eldest grandson, had somehow gotten lost on finding the place where Thomas and his future wife were to marry and hold the reception afterwards, a phone call from Melanie had informed Melinda that her and James had suddenly ran out of road after hiring a car! Was it funny then? Absolutely not, both Melinda and her party, and Melanie and James, were at tenterhooks finding their way back to somewhere, some landmark, a place one of them had recognised. Thankfully, it was the day before the actual wedding ceremony, rather than the actual day. A small recompense, any roads.

Chapter Seventeen

Melinda had reached the spot in her travelling that she had discovered, as of yesterday. Deciding to continue down the path along the coast towards what had looked like civilisation, she secured landmarks in her head, just in case. Directions had never been one of her strong points, even when Peter was around, but now alone she would have no-one to blame but herself. The onus would definitely be on her and she was nervous, very nervous.

The constant flow of people walking up and down the coastal path had meant that Melinda was indeed walking the right way, hadn't it? They couldn't all be lost! She hadn't totally convinced herself, but continued to walk slowly anyway, taking in the views around her with each and every step she made. Scenes of blue skies, blue sea with rolling waves crashing into the huge rocks on the shore below. With the sun attempting to show its face from behind the clouds, another hot and humid day was looking promising.

Stopping at the first stone bench, she parked herself on it, facing the sea and the rocky shore. The phone had Melinda clicking away, taking in the breath-taking landscape, and proof that she was actually there. It wasn't an illusion, she was there in body, though alone. Melinda wasn't hallucinating, and she was trying to be independent. Telling herself that being without Peter would take time and she would get used to it eventually, Melinda had only temporarily believed it.

If Melinda's husband had been there with her, he would have taken in the area positively and been drinking in the atmosphere, waiting for the sun to come out to play. Bathing in the hot rays whilst settled on the sun loungers around the pool, or walking around the shops and bars, Peter had relaxed completely whilst on a sunshine holiday. Looking up to the sky, Melinda had so hoped he was with her, taking everything in.

Moving on, she continued walking, passing others venturing back the other way. With her purse in her beach bag, and the name of the hotel instilled in her mind, finding a taxi for the return journey shouldn't be that difficult if she did get completely lost, should it? Passing another stone bench and yet another, Melinda stopped whilst watching a young couple bent over looking at something, something that was moving quickly between the rocks and the path.

Stopping herself and saying hello to the young couple, they pointed to the tiny chipmunks hovering around the bench and the rocks. The young man was giving them cucumber slices which the nifty creatures were picking up promptly, before running back to the rocks with their food tightly in their mouths. As one chipmunk left, another replaced it, looking dolefully at the young man, wanting the food offering for him or her.

The young man had offered Melinda a few slices of cucumber to feed them with. She had taken them, and thanked the couple. The little creatures were adorable, she'd never seen them before, not on the coast running wild that was; in a zoo or similar maybe, but that was all.

With her offerings demolished, Melinda continued walking and promised to bring some food with her when she embarked on today's route again. The creatures were apparent all along the coastal path, and even more so when she had arrived at a town called Caleta de Fuste. The chipmunks were there in abundance, all running up to visitors hoping for morsels of food. Wild creatures turning into tame ones, with many visitors obliging them with foodstuffs in their bags. Melinda remained focused on them for ages, after finding another stone bench to sit on.

As Melinda focused on the hotels around her, the rocky structure in front of her that led to the clear blue sea, had somehow appeared somewhere she had recognised. Melinda had stayed there before. The cogs turned in her brain, over and over, before realising that Peter and Melinda, along with Melanie and James, had holidayed in the hotel behind her a few years back. A lovely break in the sunshine, allowing Peter to tan his pure white skin and giving him a healthy glow. Melinda's husband had lost a lot of weight due to his illness, but he could still function normally with plenty of rest and relaxation. Fuerteventura had given him that.

Visualising the holiday then and the places they had discovered, Melinda tried to recall routes they all had taken. Landmarks of yesterday recapturing today. Melanie and James were joining her in a few days' time for a weeks' break from work and Bristol, Melinda was so looking forward to seeing them. Having a more than genuine reason to rediscover her roots of then, she continued walking along the coast and noticed a sign for the marina.

The marina was well remembered for the glass fronted refreshment bar overlooking the clear blue sea, with both Peter and Melinda relaxing in the silence whilst watching the birds flying above. The planes hovered over the marina at regular intervals, aiming for the airport and adding more visitors to the beautiful area called Fuerteventura. Small boats passing by, as and when, adding a picture postcard photograph and confirmation of a totally relaxing atmosphere.

As Melinda walked the recognisable paths, she had found a table overlooking the sea, ordering a large latte, and removing her notebook and pen from her beach bag. Inspiration had suddenly struck her, and words were quickly scribbled down before she had forgotten them. The chipmunks had a mention, the first encounter at any roads. There were bound to be a lot more written about the inquisitive little creatures. Melinda had loved seeing them and there would be a lot more times in her month there, to fully investigate the characteristics of the seemingly tame and timid rodents.

A second latte was ordered and she continued to write, page after page; suddenly ideas as to how to continue her novel was infiltrating her mind. Melinda's thoughts process had been woken up and she smiled to herself. About time, she had said silently in her head.

Peter had been in absolute heaven when they had sat there together, forgetting his illness and revelling in the glory of the views in and around them. Memories to treasure and be thankful for, a vision never to be taken away. Melinda hadn't forgotten how much her husband had devoured the peace and tranquillity. She so hoped that he was happy where he was now.

Melinda had paid for her beverages and walked around the other areas of the marina slowly, realising that a particular part of it had changed, a pool added since their last visit. Not for human beings, but a dolphin and sea lion enclosure, for them to show off their tricks to the public watching. They had appeared to be resting as Melinda passed by, show times listed nearer the pool itself. Something else to remember in her now full brain. Additions to her book were now fixed in her head and her stomach was rumbling, she'd required food urgently.

Finding an eatery nearby, Melinda sat on a vacant table and studied the menu. Evening meal back in the hotel would seriously oblige her digestive system, so a light snack was more than ample for the time being. Nachos and cheese with several dips on the side had sounded good, along with a refreshing orange juice. Melinda had eaten her dish of food slowly, ordering a second orange juice, and once again scribbling more pages to add to her novel. The snack was delicious and there would definitely be a return journey, probably with Melanie and James.

The large beach area, much larger than she had recalled, now included a camel or two, there to take visitors on their backs for a ride, for a fee that was. Melinda had already experienced a ride on the humped backed animals, years back; in Lanzarote, one of their three holidays in the part of the Canary Islands that Peter had loved. Cactus Jack's establishment had welcomed Peter every evening there, his voice on the karaoke had become regular entertainment for the duration of their breaks abroad.

A meal, several alcoholic drinks, late nights compulsory; the karaoke antics had Peter dropping his trousers and putting on a poncho and Mexican hat whilst singing The Wonder of

You, a song by none other than his idol, Elvis Presley. With other singers entering the stage as the song had come to an end, they had pulled the poncho from him, leaving him stood there in his underpants. What a site for sore eyes! Peter had enjoyed every minute of it.

A shopping mall, again something new to the area since Melinda's last visit, had her browsing around the shops inside the covered area, but not before ordering another latte and lapping up the sun's ray outside. With no clouds in site, the yellow sun above was working its magic, sitting outside was mandatory in the warm heat. A parasol ensured that visitors hadn't gotten burnt by the sun, though. All good on the western front. Melinda was finding pleasure in her investigation of Caleta de Fuste, delighting in the places visited and recognised from their vacation years before.

It had been time to return to her hotel and knowing how far it was to walk back, following her route there backwards, she'd needed to start now. Not a lot had been purchased as keepsakes, there was plenty of time for that. Overall, the day had appeared beneficial, especially with her sister and partner joining her soon. There was still a lot to see around the vicinity, but do as the Romans do; Rome wasn't built in a day!

Walking back slowly, encountering the cute chipmunks again, another cold drink was required before reaching the hotel. The Irish bar hadn't appeared too busy, so, she had entered the establishment and paid for a large coke, carrying it outside to a vacant bench in the sunshine.

Melinda had actually achieved something so unexpected for her, well out of her comfort zone. She had walked into a bar on her own and bought a drink. What was happening to her?

Conversation between locals there, ex-pats I think they are known as. Residents of the UK, now swapping the miserable weather and lifestyle for a life in the almost consistent sunshine. Winters filled with warm weather, whilst the UK was shivering in the cold wet climate. They were the sensible ones. Could Melinda live abroad, away from her family. She hadn't thought so.

Bingo was due to be played an hour later and the two ladies Melinda was talking to, had asked her if she would be partaking. Loving the game, she had declined, but had said that maybe on the next game, a few days further down the line, she would seriously consider it. Conversation with the two ladies had left her feeling happy and contented as she entered the hotel, and her home for the foreseeable future.

Melinda was now feeling tired, what with the walking and the hot sun. Time for a shower and a few hours relaxing on the sofa, before evening meal was opened in the restaurant. She wasn't going to miss that. After showering, she had sent some photos back home, to Stephanie, Drew and the boys. The oldest grandchild had loved the photos of the chipmunks, wanting to see them for himself. Wishing he was there with his grandma, Melinda would have more than welcomed him there with her. The boys' were always good company, for an older family member like Melinda.

A meow had been heard as Melinda had made herself a cup of tea, her feline friend had wanted to come in. Opening the door, allowing the black and white moggy to enter, she had immediately settled herself on Melinda's lap. Recalling Cleo, her cat from back home, sadly no longer around; at twenty years of age, Cleo was always sat on her lap or on her shoulder. She was a tabby though, not black and white, but still as adorable. She had owned a black and white cat before Cleo, who had passed away at the age of fifteen. Her youngest brother had named her Badger, due to her colouring.

Melinda had opened her laptop, followed by her notebook. Typing her scribbled words, she quickly transferred them to her novel. Further inspirational moments had entered her head and several more words were added to the manuscript. Ideas had begun to emerge at last and Melinda's smiles confirmed how she was feeling, elated. Suddenly she had felt alive, so happy that the words were now flowing, giving her a reason to continue with the novel that had been put aside to care for her ill husband. He had, and always would have come first.

The cat had decided to climb the stairs to the spare bed, so Melinda had turned on the television and watched the soaps showing; the ones she had followed back home religiously. A drama series that she had been following, was on later that evening. She could be back from the evening meal to watch it, but hadn't booked the vacation to remain in the bungalow watching television, she'd reminded herself. It was playing up a bit again, a stop off at the reception for the maintenance staff to check it out was something she'd needed to do.

Pleased with her accomplishments so far, thoughts of spending the following day around the pool and the hotel, maybe an hour in the Jacuzzi at some point; it was an option, and seriously considered. Whilst calling at the reception, a time was booked for the luxurious bubble bath for the next day, along with a visit from a maintenance person to check out the television whilst she was in the restaurant, eating her evening meal.

Melinda's stomach was full to brimming with the cuisine of the evening, and an early return to her bungalow to watch the drama episode she'd been following had happened. There were no seating areas free in the bar, so she'd returned to her bungalow immediately after eating her meal. The television had now been replaced with a similar one, but the same malfunction had still caused the interference noted on the previous set. Deciding to watch it regardless, bed had summoned afterwards, with the resident moggy keeping her company yet again.

Chapter Eighteen

The Jacuzzi was a welcome surprise the next day, in the afternoon spot that was vacant when booked the evening before. A large bubble bath full of boiling water, 38 degrees the temperature had registered. Having the luscious and soothing bath for a whole hour to herself had made her feel like royalty, special even. She'd usually shared a Jacuzzi with strangers, with them going from the large heated pool to the Jacuzzi and back, usually followed by a stint in the sauna and then a cold shower. Having locked the door behind her, Melinda had spent the whole hour totally relaxed, the effervescent pumps soothing her stomach area, the place she had been cut open to remove tummy fat which was expertly used to create a new breast, after losing her own to a mastectomy.

The plastic surgeon was such a perfectionist, a young Asian doctor who commended herself on detail, imperfections wouldn't do. For anyone who hadn't known Melinda personally, they would have been completely in the dark as regards to her medical history. There were no scars visible, even in a swimsuit. If she had stood in front of someone stark naked, then that would have been a different matter completely. The tattoo printed on the nipple area had almost disappeared, faded a long time ago. She wasn't prepared to go through any more surgery, so a faded nipple it was; who was going to see it anyway?

As Melinda stood up and tore herself away from the bubbling water, a return visit (more than one) would definitely be booked further down the line. Not having a bath in her bungalow, there was no question about it. She would be making a date with the Jacuzzi once again. Returning the key to the receptionist, reluctantly, Melinda thanked her before heading for a vacant sun lounger and a cool drink. Would the paperback come out of her beach bag or her notepad with new inspirational thoughts to scribble about? As it turned out, it was a bit of both.

Melinda had noticed a leaflet on the reception desk, regarding a free bus into Caleta de Fuste, and had asked where to get the transport from. She had passed the directions indicated the day before, and was seriously thinking about trying it out the following morning. Melanie and James were due to arrive at the hotel later that evening, so it would be interesting to know where the bus had stopped in the town, for them as much as herself.

Early the next morning, Melinda had walked to the hotel mentioned by the receptionist, just a few minutes' walk away. She'd eaten breakfast early and was eager to explore a bit more. Weather wise, the clouds were still keeping the sun covered, hopefully it wouldn't be too long before the clouds would disappear completely. There was no bus stop sign outside the hotel, but there were a few people stood on the corner, so Melinda had asked if they were waiting for the free bus. They were, though when it had arrived on time, it was actually a coach.

There were a few people already on the coach and Melinda walked onto it, sitting halfway along, hoping to follow others when getting off the transport itself. She hadn't a clue which direction the vehicle would pursue, but hoped for the best. Initial landmarks when reaching the town the other day, could guide her as to where the coach was heading; Melinda had her fingers crossed on that score.

As more bodies climbed the steps of the coach, Melinda's journey had begun. The coach passed a few landmarks, pulling in for people to mount or dismount, but the majority of travellers had remained in their seats. She had followed suit and stayed put, for now. The vehicle had passed the shopping precinct, somewhere she had already fully checked out. It was the shops on the various side roads that Melinda had wanted to find, an area she had recalled from her previous holiday there. Melinda had remembered a large pharmacist on a square, with eateries and other shops centred around it. Not having discovered it as yet, she had hoped to see a familiar reminder as the coach continued its route around the town. Anything would have done!

The pharmacist was somewhere found for both Peter and Melanie, Melinda's husband requiring antibiotics for his illness, and Melanie due to a throbbing toothache that was causing annoying pain. It had been minutes away from their hotel then, so couldn't be difficult to find, could it? As the coach stopped outside a large hotel, centred around a golf course, a few people had disembarked. The queue of people waiting to get on it would fill the vehicle up completely, with others having to wait for the next available coach.

Melinda had decided to disembark, thinking that she couldn't be far from the shopping area she was trying to hunt out. How wrong she was, walking around the golf course and ending up outside the shopping precinct of earlier. Melinda's worst subject in school had been geography, not much had changed as her age had progressed. Directions, as far as Melinda was concerned was indeed diabolical.

Walking through the shopping mall once again, she continued along the beach promenade, passing all the areas she had already discovered beforehand. Passing the camels once more, a cool refreshing drink was urgently wanted, and stopping at an outside bar she had ordered a large orange juice, refreshing and including the zesty bits. Deciding to give up on pursuing her original reason for catching the free coach that morning, the chipmunk trail was now being walked, back to her hotel well in time for her imminent arrivals. What a waste of time, Melinda hadn't discovered anything new and was a little disappointed with herself.

A message from Melanie had indicated that they were now on the shuttle bus awaiting the driver, and their arrival to the hotel itself. The journey from the airport to the hotel was a mere fifteen minutes, but after waiting for an hour or so, until all passengers were there in person, they had landed almost ninety minutes later. With Melinda having arrived earlier in the week, she was able to enlighten them on most things around the complex. They had been given an upgrade, and a large self-contained apartment on the first floor, huge in comparison to Melinda's bungalow. Melinda was more than happy with her accommodation and her friendly moggy keeping her company during the evenings.

Holidays with Melanie and James were frequent over the years, weekly breaks in the sunshine relaxing and topping up their tans. There had been two vacations, single weekly breaks spent with just Melanie and Melinda. Gran Canaria, one of them, was a small bungalow painted a vivid bright green, but on the inside it was more than habitable. Not luxury, neither of them had expected it to be, not with the price they had paid for the break abroad. Melanie had moved onto the couch in the living area after a few days there, due to a colony of ants deciding to occupy her bed; there wasn't room for Melanie as well. It hadn't deterred them from continuing the holiday at all. A memorable reason to laugh, as opposed to cry, and Peter hadn't minded his wife and sister-in-law going on holiday without him. He'd needed to work to pay the bills. James, on the other hand had appeared envious of the two girls going away alone, sulking in the UK when Melanie had spoken to him.

The other break had occurred in Calella, another part of Spain. An average accommodation, no complaints at first, until discovering the lack of air conditioning, and night-times spent roasting in the intense heat indoors. The patio doors were open to its maximum whilst trying to sleep of an evening. With Melinda having to be careful with the rays of the sun, due to her breast cancer diagnosis, covered up with a hat, sunglasses and a beach robe, people around must have been laughing at her and her dress attire. The temperature was verging on thirty five degrees!

As the days had passed, the patio furniture on the balcony had somehow moved frequently. Initially blaming it on the cleaners, a voice from a young female had Melanie checking things out on the balcony one night. Watching a young girl climb over from the next balcony onto Melanie and Melinda's, then climbing onto the balcony the other side of them, had Melinda's sister asking questions. Reassuring them both that she hadn't stolen anything, but wanted to see the occupants next door to them, being on the fifth floor of the building, had appeared a tad precarious. Woe behold, if she had fallen to the ground. Teenagers never seemed to see the danger!

Holidays with her sister, with or without their spouses, always had reason to laugh and remember with a smile. Highlights of a unique break with a few catastrophes had made the experiences even more special. Who would want a boring break where nothing exciting had happened and bedtime was earlier than when at home? Not Melinda, the oddities had well outweighed normality. Living at its best, for sure.

Back to the here and now, Melanie and James had moved into their apartment satisfactorily and food and drink were next on the agenda. Melinda headed the way to the restaurant, finding a table for four, and tucking into the food on offer. James, a tall person with a large appetite, had probably eaten four courses to Melanie and Melinda's two. The food on offer was there to eat, with either small or large appetites. The bar lounge was also there to sup up the alcohol and Melinda felt much more comfortable drinking with companions, namely Melanie and James.

As per usual, vacant seats in the lounge area were scarce, so outside again it was. The entertainment, if you could call it that, could be heard from outside the lounge, so none of them were missing out on anything; nothing at all really. Melinda had loved having them there with her, even if it was only for a week. They could do a lot in a week, discovering and reminiscing their last vacation there, in Caletta de Fuste, when Peter was there with them. He was so missed, and talked about often. Melinda had needed that, recognition that he had actually existed. Peter was adored by his family, who couldn't love him?

Late nights had become the order of the day whilst the three of them were together. Sat around the large pool, drinks flowing frequently; food in abundance, even elevenses and mid-afternoon nibbles were eaten, as well as breakfast, lunch, and dinner. Melinda couldn't eat so much every day, but for a short while, she'd managed okay. The Jacuzzi had a return visit, this time with the three of them sharing the bubbles in the pool. It hadn't seen the last of Melinda, though, that was a certainty.

The Irish bar had received a visit, an evening meal out and listening to the resident vocalist and the tunes on his guitar, he was good. The gentleman was an established singer in Fuerteventura. If it hadn't been for the vicinity of the bar's toilets, it would have definitely had a return visit. With the men's WC next to the singer, the barman had repeatedly entered the conveniences with a mop and bucket. Watching him clean up whilst listening to the music was hilarious. The male drinkers' obvious aims at the urinal was missed several times. A barrel of laughs recalling the simplest of occurrences.

A meal in the Indian restaurant on Melanie and James' last day was superb, delicious, and a welcome change from buffet food. Ironically, it was Valentine's Day, and James was escorting two ladies that evening, Melanie and Melinda. All a bit weird really, but nothing was said. Melinda had managed to eat a Sunday roast the day after they had returned to the UK. She happily sat outside in the sunshine, tucking into a chicken dinner, two glasses of white wine, and her notepad open for her to scribble in once again. Her inspiration was back, she was on form again, having written nothing at all whilst accompanying her visitors, her sister and partner.

Passing the Crazy Goat on returning to the hotel, Melinda had so wanted to enter the establishment, but couldn't do it, not on her own. She had needed to summon up the courage to talk to others, others holidaying on their own. With James' help, they had befriended two elderly couples, lovely people, with one of the couples residing next door to her bungalow. Tony and Doreen were a joy to talk to, usually sat outside the lounge bar after the evening meal was finished. With their friends Walter and Gill, Melinda would sit with them for one or two alcoholic beverages, before walking back with them to their bungalows. She could converse with them easily, and was made to feel at home sat with them of an evening.

A hello and a wave to recognised faces, those there since Melinda had inhabited her bungalow, realising her ability to be a little more confrontational. Couples on tables next to her in the restaurant became a source of conversation whilst eating their food. Not visitors she could amalgamate with during the day, but recognisable faces to at least conduct a small conversation with. Melinda was suddenly enjoying herself, along with feeling a part of the community, eager to help others when required.

Taking photographs of friends in the water, the ice cool pool, and it was very cold; talking to them about anything or nothing. Guiding newcomers to areas they weren't aware of, and general conversation between people at intervals. Sun lounge neighbours were there to communicate between tanning their bodies in the hot sunshine, male and female. Melinda had suddenly felt a part of the complex and its residents that would come and go, some there for a month, similar to Melinda. She was finally revelling in the month long holiday that should have included Peter, her husband of forty-three years.

Chapter Nineteen

With Melinda's confidence now at its best, her enthusiasm at exploring the island further had gone into overdrive. Browsing through the excursions available she had booked up two trips, one to an area further up the coast, namely Corralejo. A busy town with more shops to visit, as well as a beautiful marina and plenty of eateries around. The coach was to pick her up outside the hotel in a few days' time. Melinda was looking forward to it, though a little apprehensive.

The other trip booked, had needed Melinda's confidence to blossom even more. She had paid to spend the day in Lanzarote, crossing the water in a ferry early in the morning to allow plenty of leisure time in another of the Canary Islands, one familiar to Melinda. The excursion was booked for the following week. Melinda had to pluck up the courage to realise a day in Lanzarote, but firstly, the coach trip to Corralejo was looming. Could she go through with them, on her own?

Never one to waste money, Melinda stood outside the hotel with others awaiting coaches for different excursions, as well as the one Melinda had booked to go on. As she climbed the steps onto the coach, she sat in the middle again; not a person to want to be in the limelight, middle way was more than appropriate. Listening carefully to the courier, she had described a stop to the sandy area en route to Corralejo before stopping in the town itself. Times were mentioned as to how long everyone had to explore and shop, before catching the return coach, and back to Fuerteventura; in time for evening meal in the hotel's restaurant.

Gazing out of the window as the coach pursued its journey, Melinda had laughed inwardly to herself, noting a road taken next to the hotel had been one she had walked up for a long period of time, just days earlier. She had rested at a bus stop for a while before walking all the way back to her original footmark, the pretty coastal area overlooking the sea beyond, her first encounter after arriving at the hotel. As the coach had entered the road, there in full view was the bus stop she had sat at, whilst talking to a young lad native to the area, a polite youngster waiting for the bus himself. His broken English was applaudable, as he tried to converse with Melinda, knowing she was a tourist visiting his homeland. Melinda had come full circle, but hadn't realised it. What was it that Melinda had mentioned about being awful at geography in school? There was the proof, pure Melinda style.

The fifteen minute stop, walking carefully over the sand dunes, her phone in her hand to take photographs of the gorgeous golden sand, devoid of anything else around. Picture perfect with the sun shining in all its glory, absolutely beautiful. It was just sand in reality, but the large dunes and the absence of anything else around in the vicinity had turned it into something magical, in all its innocence.

As they approached Corralejo, Melinda had taken careful note of where the coach had stopped; the spot where she was to mount the coach again on its return journey home. Instilled safely in her brain, she had four hours to herself, to explore and spend money. Melinda was looking forward to investigating another part of Fuerteventura. As she walked the length of the numerous shops around, with eateries in abundance, she'd known that the area would have been Melanie's guilty pleasure. Jewellery shops, sports shops and women's clothing with shoes and accessories; all Melinda's sister's convincing reasons to spend money. If Melanie hadn't purchased a pair of shoes whilst on holiday, there would be something wrong, seriously so. To Melanie, the purchase was compulsory and no-one had argued with her, ever.

Heading for the marina, following arrows directing the way, Melinda was pleasantly surprised. The area was awe-inspiring, absolutely stunning. Small eateries were situated overlooking the large expanse of water, with small, medium and large vessels parked up in it. People were swimming in the sea, from the small piece of golden sand directly next to the marina itself. It was beautiful, so she settled herself outside one of the small eateries. An establishment with views directly over the fabulous water, a definite photo required.

She had ordered nachos and dips yet again, a large latte, and revelled in the sights in front of her. Absolute heaven, recalling seaside towns in the UK equally as pretty. Devon and Cornwall had seaside ports in abundance, but Fishguard in Pembrokeshire had become number one, and the best, in Peter and Melinda's eyes. She'd had to order another latte as the notebook and pen had planted itself on the table, there to be scribbled in. Words had failed her as the pen had noted down everything seen with her own eyes.

More shops were browsed until Melinda had reached an eatery, sadly not open, but outside had secured a life-like image of the one and only, Elvis Presley. Taking a photo of the statue, one with the idol playing a guitar, had in Melinda's eyes confirmed that her husband was there with her. She had suddenly shivered in the intense heat, convinced that Peter was seeing the statue of his and thousands of others' singing sensation, a voice never to be forgotten. If Peter was still alive, a photo with Melinda's husband stood by him, would have been compulsory. No question about it.

Melinda had purchased a few souvenirs, spending monies more on food and refreshments that bric-a-brac. Not wanting to lose her way back to the coach stop, she hadn't ventured too far from the beaten track. A coffee bar local to the stop had finished her shopping spree, before queuing for the return journey back to the hotel. Was Melinda pleased with herself? Absolutely, she'd deserved a pat on the back for being so courageous. Knowing the travelling to Lanzarote would be a different ball game altogether, she was well prepared for her next adventure.

The upcoming excursion to Lanzarote hadn't been far away, and the free coach was used on a regular basis. She was now well educated as to where the coach had stopped, and had indeed found the square and the shops on the side roads. She had also become acquainted with a lady from Glasgow, called Pat. Pat had spoken to her whilst outside of the lounge bar in the hotel one evening. With two brandy's in her hands, she had asked if she could sit with Melinda. Melinda had put down her phone as conversation had begun. If Melinda was honest, the Glaswegian accent had her not fully understanding parts of the conversation. She was also waiting for her husband, friend, whoever joining them, until she had realised that Pat was actually on her own and had received two drinks at the bar, saving her returning too quickly for a refill. A good move, definitely. She was all there!

From then on, for the week Pat was there, they had spent time together. Walking the chipmunk trail, buying an English breakfast out and gambling a few Euros in the bookmakers attached to the eatery. The Crazy Goat had found them spending the evenings there, as opposed to the lounge bar. The entertainment was so much better there, excellent singers and an atmosphere Peter would have excelled in, and thoroughly delighted in. Pat had saved the day, giving Melinda a few evenings outside of the hotel, in a locals pub full of noise and excitement. She still couldn't understand some of the conversation between them, but had nodded anyway.

Pat was seventy years of age, a few years older than Melinda, but her antics and personality was infectious. You couldn't help but like her, Peter would have loved her as a holidaymaker to spend time with, she was a laugh a minute. Eating in the restaurant had now included Pat at her table. Tony and Doreen had smiled, looking at them both, knowing that Melinda had found a companion, someone to spend time with. Her apartment was directly next to the reception area, so Melinda would call for Pat as she headed for the restaurant and food. 'Is Pat coming out to play?' had echoed in Melinda's mind. Something Peter would have said to her with a huge grin on his face. Melinda could see him now, full of life and acting the fool in front of her, and Pat joining in with his frolicking about.

It was on the third visit to The Crazy Goat that Melinda had really experienced Pat at her best. During the evening meal, she had indulged in two white wines whilst eating her dinner. As they entered The Crazy Goat, her tipple had changed to brandy, larger than the average tot and closer to a double if Melinda had been completely honest, who was herself drinking Coca Cola. Trying to lead a conversation with the band playing known songs for others to dance to, they had both paid for four drinks, alternating every other round.

Not having a watch on, Pat had asked the time. As Melinda had glanced at her watch, it had shown the time as twenty minutes to one in the morning. Not wanting to be stopped from entering the hotel, thinking aloud, they both finished their drinks and headed for home, well the hotel any roads. As they walked across the road to the hotel, Pat had fallen in the middle of it, flat on her face. Pat was a large framed lady, and Melinda couldn't pick her up, though she had tried several times.

'Wait there Pat,' Melinda had said. 'I will go and get a few men from the bar to help.' Melinda had done just that and two of the younger men there, Scottish, of course, had followed her.

Pat was then seen crawling up the middle of the road on her hands and knees. They couldn't help but laugh, she'd looked so funny. The men managed to pick her up, allowing Melinda to catch hold of her the rest of the way. They would have escorted her to the hotel if Melinda couldn't have managed, both more than willing to help out. As they entered the hotel, she had asked Pat for her key, which Melinda's friend had obliged. Their ordeal wasn't over, there had been more to come.

Melinda couldn't open the door, the key just wouldn't work. By this time, Pat was sat on the patio chair in front of her apartment, completely inebriated. A visit to the reception desk had the male member of staff following Melinda, and thankfully for her, had had trouble opening the door himself. It wasn't Melinda's hands playing up this time, the door couldn't be opened with the key in Pat's keeping. Eventually he had managed to free the lock open, promising to sort it out properly the next day.

Melinda had ensured Pat was okay in her apartment before walking to her bungalow. Pat had waved to her and said. 'I will see you at ten-thirty tomorrow morning. Call for me.'

Ten-thirty am was too late for breakfast, but seeing the state Pat was in, the chance on her wanting breakfast the next morning would be far and few between. Melinda could manage without breakfast, no harm done there. As Melinda sat drinking a cup of tea in her bungalow the next morning, her phone had rung. Picking it up and hearing Pat's voice at the end of it, she'd asked if all was okay.

'Where are you?' Pat had asked quizzically.

'You said ten-thirty,' was Melinda's reply. 'Are you feeling okay?'

'Yes, I'm fine. Why, what happened last night?' Pat hadn't recalled anything about the evening before.

'You fell in the middle of the road on the way back to the hotel. You were crawling in the middle of it and I got help from The Crazy Goat to pick you up. You were concerned about your trousers, because they were new.' Melinda stopped for breath. 'I couldn't open your apartment door and had to get the receptionist to open it. They are going to sort the lock out later for you.'

'Oh,' had been Pat's reply, having not recalled any of it. Furthermore, she had sounded completely sober.

'I'm on my way to yours now. We can get breakfast out somewhere. I won't be long.' Melinda put down the phone, picked up her beach bag and locked the door behind her. As she trotted along to Pat's apartment a humongous laugh was let out from Melinda's mouth. Unbelievable, would anyone even contemplate what had occurred less than twelve hours ago, if she had repeated it to any sane person on the complex? It hadn't sounded feasible at all, causing Melinda to let out another giggle as she entered her friend's apartment. It would have been even worse if she'd drank alcohol too. What would have happened then? The choices thought about hadn't appeared worthy of an answer. Whoever said fun was just for teenagers were completely delusional. Two over sixties were there, betting otherwise. Melinda's cheeks were aching through the laughter. Pensioners at their best, well nearly, as far as Melinda was concerned.

It was sad seeing Pat leave for Scotland, and home. Promising to speak on Facebook, Pat was the laugh she had needed to take away the pain of losing her husband. Her life story was more complicated, as far as she could tell, but Pat had known how to live and was doing just that. As it had happened, another lady there on her own had made her presence known, and Melinda had been scheduled to show her the chipmunk trail the following day. Her name was Annie, an unknown entity Melinda would soon get to know.

Chapter Twenty

As things had turned out, Annie had already been shown the chipmunk trail by two eligible gentlemen on the complex. Not being backward at coming forward, Annie had spoken to them whilst sunbathing around the pool. As regards to being eligible though, they were due to marry the following year in a civil partnership. They had clicked with Annie immediately and were more than comfortable with her joining them during the day.

As originally planned, both Melinda and Annie went for a walk and got to know one another. She was seventy-one years of age, and married to a postman on the Isle of Skye, the Scottish accent still causing a few issues with Melinda; the quick pace of speech very similar to the Welsh people's spoken words, even when conversing in the English language. She had managed to understand her a little better than she had initially had with Pat, all good.

Annie hadn't been able to have children, so had given her love to animals instead. With three dogs and a cat, one of them had sadly passed away just days before her arrival to Fuerteventura. With no-one available to care for them, they spent holidays apart, on their own, to ensure the pets were always looked after. The docile creatures were Annie's world, with her husband, of course.

Conversation about holidays in general, Annie had, over the years, been rewarded with three or four breaks throughout each and every year since retiring. She was completely at ease travelling and discovering parts of the world on her own. It appeared that the same could be said for her husband. They had both mastered the art of holidaying alone, acknowledging that Annie's idea of a vacation was totally different to her husband's taste.

Annie's dress sense was a little outrageous, she had well stood out in the crowd. Wearing a blond hairpiece during her vacation, a face full of bold make-up, Melinda was all for people dressing the way they had felt happy with. Melinda herself, was the boring example, not standing out at all. Easy wearing clothes, not too outlandish or glitzy, everyday wear was worn without a hint of make-up and her hair pulled back into a ponytail during the day. Her hair was left loose when the evening had arose and tidy clothes worn, nothing too elaborate. Plain Jane, Melinda wasn't, but looking smart she was content with her style of dress.

Only knowing the two handsome gentlemen, and they were handsome, for a few days, Annie had already received an invitation to their civil ceremony at their home in Manchester. A matron of honour they had wanted her to be, and Annie had accepted immediately. Her husband of over twenty years was obviously used to her way of living and trusted her implicitly.

In Melinda's eyes though, her personality could have become off putting and overpowering to some; Melinda, honestly, had stressed her writing and her need to try and push her novel whilst there, expressing that she had required spending time in her bungalow or alone scribbling away in her notebook at some point. It was a goal Melinda had wanted to pursue, and although several chapters had actually been copied from her notebook to the laptop, not nearly enough accomplished as she had hoped for.

Annie had her two gentlemen as well as Melinda, so she hadn't felt that guilty. Her day in Lanzarote was forthcoming as well, just one more day before her new experience booked. The excursion had been paid for before Annie had even arrived in Fuerteventura, so she hadn't felt that she had left Annie out, not on that score.

After finishing her evening meal that night, rather than Melinda heading directly for her bungalow, or sitting with Tony and Doreen and Walter and Gill, if they were visible, she followed Annie into the lounge and copied her by sitting at the bar. Melinda hadn't felt comfortable at all, but her friend appeared to be in her element. The young host handed them both a bingo ticket, one solitary ticket; it was free though. The prize was something stupid, it had to be, they both marked the numbers as they had been called out, nevertheless.

An elderly-ish gentleman, age unknown, had stood next to Annie, seemingly chatting her up; Annie's face had lit up at the compliments she was receiving from him, and she was blushing, before he had moved next to Melinda trying to do the same to her. Not feeling comfortable, Melinda had climbed off the high bar stool after finishing her drink, relaying her apologies to her friend.

'I will see you tomorrow Annie, in the restaurant.' Melinda had said as she walked out of the lounge. Leaving her there with the very loud male person, Annie was in her element. It was definitely not Melinda's scene, not now and probably not in the future either. Peter had spoiled her, and forty-three years of marriage had shown her true committal to their relationship. Finding someone similar in Melinda's future years wasn't even thinkable right now. Lonely or not, Melinda was now on her own, and through choice. Forming another relationship was a definite no-no, especially a loud male, one she had just experienced.

Melinda stood outside the hotel early in the morning, ready for her visit to Lanzarote, Playa Blanca. The southernmost town of the Spanish island and the newest part of the municipality of Yaiza. An area neither Melinda nor Peter had experienced before. Lanzarote holidays were always spent in Costa Teguise, in the north-central part of the island. A rather windy area, but it was where Cactus Jack's bar, eatery, and karaoke extravaganza was; Peter wouldn't go anywhere else in the country, Lanzarote that was, as long as Cactus Jack's had remained in existence. A fun holiday in the wind and the sunshine was what the area had represented, in Peter's eyes alone.

The coach had set off with its holidaymakers in tow, heading for the ferry and the destination of Playa Blanca. It hadn't taken long in the coach, and the driver had given instructions as to what time to re-board the ferry on its voyage back to Fuerteventura. Leaving the holidaymakers to board the seafaring vehicle, he had said his goodbyes.

Melinda's nerves were showing trepidation, concerned as to whether she had listened properly to the instructions, and her fear at missing the ferry back and as a consequence the coach, to the hotel she was staying at. Had Melinda bitten off more than she could chew? As she found a seat on the ferry, looking out to the sea all around, Melinda would soon find out, wouldn't she!

The sun was hotter than ever as Melinda had disembarked the seaworthy vehicle, noting the landmarks in her head, of both the ferry itself and the stopping point of the vehicle; also ensuring her watch was indeed at its correct time. Melinda had five hours to explore, eat and drink, and take pictures of yet another Canary island, an area never ventured to before. The braveness she had felt booking up the excursion a week earlier, had now heeded a large amount of self-doubt in her head. Was Melinda still confident and courageous now that she had landed so far away from her hotel? No, she wasn't. Not at all. Silently calling to her husband for help, she had no choice but to do her uttermost and experience the excursion at its best.

Initially following others in front of her, who probably hadn't a clue where they were going either, she had studied a few of the people getting off the ferry and their mode of dress. There was a couple, well Melinda had presumed anyway; the lady was in a wheelchair, with the man pushing her, a definite two people for her to remember as the time would elapse. She hadn't spoken to them as yet, not knowing whether she actually would do.

Melinda was walking a pedestrian path overlooking the turquoise blue sea and the golden sand next to it. Large luxurious hotels were evident as she continued walking, as well as the odd souvenir shop and small eateries overlooking the view Melinda couldn't take her eyes from. With the sun really hotting up, Melinda had turned around, walking back the way she had come. There was an eatery that had looked very inviting, with a vacant table and two chairs overlooking the fabulous scenery, there for Melinda to take occupancy of. Bodies were frolicking in the pools of water opposite, before it merged into the sea beyond. Absolutely breath-taking and so mesmerising, beautiful and beyond beautiful. She was in absolute heaven, drinking up the brilliance of it all.

She had loved what she was seeing, evident as the mobile phone had taken picture after picture, after picture. Peter would have excelled in just sitting there, eating it all up slowly, totally in his element. Ordering a toasted sandwich and a large latte, the notepad and pen was put on the table as she had waited for her food and beverage, with the pen constantly scribbling away, word after word. Inspiration had taken hold of her, the glorious day and atmosphere working its magic for her.

The food had been finished and a second large latte ordered. Melinda still scribbled away, the most she had written since beginning her holiday, and her mind was filling up with ideas for the novel, good ones at that. With the obvious high grade hotels around, the expense would have been more that Melinda and Peter could ever have afforded. It was more than obvious, but was still okay to dream and admire. That hadn't cost a penny!

A two or three star hotel would have included them, purely for the price, but in reality Peter would not have wanted a top-notch environment. Clean and average, down to earth, Peter's ideal vacation. Working class he was, and completely at home with his class in society, not wishing to aim any higher in life. Posh was okay for others, their choice, but winning the lottery wouldn't have changed him, not at all. He would have still wanted to help others repairing or doing up their houses, for a mere chat and unlimited cups of tea.

As Melinda stood up from the table, putting her notepad and pen back in her beach bag, she spoke to the couple behind her, seemingly sat in the shade. The sun completely hidden from where they were seated. Offering them her now vacant seats and table, to infiltrate the rays onto their bodies, rather than Melinda's, the lady there had thanked her, but had said she'd preferred to be in the shade. She then asked Melinda if she was writing a book, and a lengthy conversation had evolved about her published novels and the one she was now trying to complete. A lovely talk between strangers and so endearing, Melinda had smiled, elated, as she continued her walk.

Deciding to find the marina, Melinda followed signs and through more luck than judgement had found it, discovered the pretty area known for the views of the water and the fabulous boats in all its glory, all centred around the harbour itself. There were several shops along the way, and she bought a sleeveless dress she had liked, even though she really hadn't needed anything else to wear. Her wardrobes at home were full to bursting, not that that had stopped her if something had taken her fancy. She was on holiday, her reasoning. Melinda was allowed and Peter had never refused her, if he had been with her that was.

A sit down, a refreshing drink, a few more photos taken. There was still an hour or so to go before heading back for the ferry back to Fuerteventura. Melinda hadn't wanted to shop anymore, so walked back to the path she'd walked in the beginning. There was an Irish bar there, a large and spacious one with plenty of outside seating, and vacant areas in abundance. Ordering a large pineapple juice and lemonade with plenty of ice cubes, Melinda relaxed. As she dreamt about the past and thought about Peter, a song had played loudly from the inside of the premises, echoing loudly outside. A song so recognisable. It was none other than Elvis Presley, singing The Wonder of You.

Goosebumps had suddenly covered her arms and she had shivered in the intensely hot sun. Peter was there with her, Melinda was certain of it. He was surely watching over her, keeping her safe. Pure coincidence probably, but she had convinced herself otherwise. He would be there in spirit, if not in body. A smile had erupted as she drank her refreshingly cool pineapple cocktail, and a reason to continue on her travels was now obligatory. Peter would be with her, somewhere along the road, at some point in time. She wasn't on her own at all.

The couple that Melinda had landmarked as she had disembarked the ferry, were there at the beginning of the queue for the return voyage. The ferry wasn't there as yet, so she spoke to the couple, about everything and nothing in particular. Melinda had been wrong, not unusual on that score. They were neighbours, friends, and holiday buddies. Having tried at a relationship, something that hadn't worked out, they had vowed to remain friends and continue with their escapades as true companions, but without the romance. How endearing, Melinda was touched, almost dropping a tear from her eye. *Happiness can be met*, she had thought. Melinda had needed to remember that for the future.

On finally reaching their hotel, Melinda would often stop and talk if seeing them in the complex, at any given time. Times when she had actually espied them passing by. A lovely lesson the couple had brought to light. The world wasn't always bad, there were fairy-tales amongst the rough and difficult periods, and nothing was ever perfect.

Chapter Twenty-One

With Melinda's month coming to an end, Annie had continued to keep her company most of the time, when the boys' weren't around, and when she wasn't typing away in her bungalow. The novel was coming along swimmingly and Melinda had had no idea where her thoughts were going as far as the story was concerned. It was happening though, and she had not wanted to lose sight of the inspirations now clearly set in her head. Losing her motivational chapters, filled with a hopeful romance, intrigue, and friendly encounters, she'd needed to be on the ball. Fuerteventura and Lanzarote had opened her mind with several optional conclusions, all good on the writing score. Melinda was pleased with her efforts. The black and white moggy was still there with her, keeping her company during the evenings.

With her sister and brother-in-law now in Caleta de Fuste, Annie had asked Melinda if she had wanted to meet them, and enjoy a meal out together. A positive nod from Melinda had them catching the free coach into the town, a ride used as a matter of course now. Meeting up in the enclosed shopping mall, Annie's sister was recognised instantly by her similar features. Two peas in a pod, as the saying goes. There was no doubt about their relationship to one another; as was with Melinda and Melanie as regards to their family likeness.

It wasn't a first time to the area for Annie's sister and brother-in-law, they appeared to know their way around perfectly. Finding an eatery amongst an abundance of small shops, an area Melinda had discovered herself whilst there, on her own surprisingly. Melinda had chosen a prawn salad, not recalling the others' options on the menu, to be exact. The food was good, four satisfied customers. Annie and her sister's tipple was a large glass of wine each, Melinda was happy with water, determined not to become dehydrated in the hot and humid heat from the sun's rays. A large beer, more than one, being drunk by the male member of the foursome, Annie's brother-in-law.

A telephone call from Annie's mobile phone, had her getting up from the table and walking away, very suddenly. Her sister had known something was up, and followed her in quick succession. Conversation between the two remaining at the table was informative, interesting, and in retrospect, helpful as far as Annie was concerned. Her animals were her life, not having children, and Melinda knew to tread carefully where her pets were concerned.

Annie returned wiping her eyes, telling them that her pet dog, Tanya, had, on the vet's advice been put to sleep. She had suffered the same illnesses as her recent pet that had passed away, a week or so earlier. Melinda was almost in tears herself, and knew nothing about her dogs apart from seeing their pictures on Annie's phone. Realising that she needed to be there keeping her company, she was so glad that she had agreed to the meet up. She couldn't bring the tiny animals back to life, but Melinda was there for support.

As Annie's family left to return to their hotel, the remaining ladies browsed the local shops there, with Annie purchasing two pairs of pantaloons, women's baggy trousers gathered at the ankles. Definitely not Melinda's choice of attire, but Annie had loved them. Melinda had needed to buy a small bag, small enough for hand luggage on the plane home. Nothing had spoken to her as yet, so she would look whilst on her own, knowing exactly what she was searching for.

As they walked back via the chipmunk trail, it had to be, nothing else would suffice. The timid little creatures would cheer Annie up no end, and they did. Melinda's friend was smiling between the tears, they seemed to have that effect on humans. With Melinda carrying a few biscuits in her beach bag, picked up whilst eating breakfast, the little things were in for a treat. They weren't feeding the ducks, they were feeding the chipmunks. Who would believe them back in the UK?

Reaching the hotel, Annie had excused herself and headed back to her apartment, post haste. Emotions high, the tears would be flowing for one of her babies. Her husband had tried his best to wait until Annie had returned home, before letting Tanya fall to sleep, free from pain, but it would have been cruel to allow her to suffer any longer. He had the pet pooch's interest at heart. Annie had so wished that she was there to say goodbye.

Meeting in the restaurant for evening meal, Melinda was careful regarding conversation, not wanting to upset her unnecessarily. With her make-up hiding the redness of her eyes, Annie was coping well, considering. The boys' were taking her to the Irish bar afterwards, so Melinda had one drink in the bar, sitting outside, before retiring to her bungalow and copying her scribbled words not yet transferred to the laptop.

The final few days had become much of the same, topping up her tan, having her final hour of luxury in the Jacuzzi, soaking up the effervescent bubbles whilst thinking about things; her novel, her final gifts needing to purchase, and recalling her holiday and its success without her husband by her side. The chipmunks were rewarded with one more lunch of biscuits from the breakfast bar whilst Melinda had hunted out successfully, the travel bag she desperately required. The one brought over initially had broken, so the purchase was absolutely essential.

As she waited outside for the coach to take her to the airport, very early in the morning, she had told Annie not to get up to see her off, mainly because of the departure time. Melinda hadn't wanted any fuss either, was the long and tall of it. They did exchange Facebook details to be able to stay in touch, and still converse that way now.

All in all, the holiday was a hit, a resounding success. If asked to consider another month away, she wouldn't hesitate to book a similar type of vacation again. For now though, Melinda was only glad that she had survived it, as well as showing her ability to go it alone; something so alien for the last forty-five years of her life. It had indeed been a gamble chosen to honour one of both Peter and Melinda's goals for retirement and the future beyond, and thankfully it hadn't turned into a total disaster.

James and Melanie were picking her up from the airport, and Melinda was staying a few days with them, before travelling back to Wales and her home. It would be almost five weeks since she had left her house unoccupied, and at the moment Melinda wasn't in any hurry to return to her sometimes lonely existence. She had missed her family members; her daughter, son-in-law, and the two boys, her grandsons. That was obvious, the grandchildren were central to her existing, and being needed, something absolutely crucial to Melinda managing her future, something that was unknown and strange to her as yet. Melinda's son and his family's visits were far and few between, their choice in the crux of things, and she'd not wanted to interfere there.

Losing Peter had meant that her reasons for actually believing that she was important, had now disintegrated into obscurity, no longer there. The nursing part of a sick husband was a twenty-four hour job, without any time to feel sorry for oneself at all. Melinda hadn't only lost her soulmate, but also the job that looking after him had entailed. With so much time on her hands, life had appeared boring, lonely, and more importantly had made her feel unwanted and useless.

Stephanie and Drew had important full-time jobs, as well as two young boys to bring up. Their lives were hectic, and although Melinda did have a child-care role in picking up the youngest from school a few days a week, they didn't really have time to listen and understand how Melinda was actually feeling without Peter, Stephanie's dad. Stephanie was grieving, no question about it; Melinda was also grieving, for her old life back as well as her long-time partner, her husband.

Amanda was there, Melinda couldn't have coped without her, but she had her own family to be among, too. Others had managed well after losing relatives, Melinda would also manage, given time. Not one to give up on anything she had believed in, Stephanie's mother was putting on a brave front, probably too brave. Honestly, this was the hardest thing Melinda had ever needed to encounter, and at times she'd not wanted to believe that Peter would never walk through the door again.

Whilst staying with James and Melanie, Melinda had concentrated on her novel whilst they were at work, and continued life in general when they were home. Apart from bedtime, she had company with people on a similar level to her own. Family members who understood how Melinda worked. It had helped her to get through the loss, recalling memories of Peter that she herself had forgotten. The laughter and smiles somehow released the pent up feelings she was frightened to bring out, for why she wasn't sure. Laughing about Peter's habits and characteristics had felt so good all of a sudden.

James and Melanie had driven her back to her humble abode in Wales, staying a few hours before driving back to Bristol themselves, their home. Melinda's thoughts were now uppermost in her mind; her long escapade and her enjoyment at actually achieving something absolutely necessary to her future, so crucial. Her head was still in holiday mode as she opened her suitcase and loaded some of the worn and dirty clothes into the washing machine. Others already washed whilst out there, in Fuerteventura, had remained in the clothes carrier to put away in her wardrobe later, or sometime the following day. It hadn't mattered which.

Melinda, as a child, was never one to feel completely confident about anything (or herself) that much. A middle of the road pupil, neither pretty nor ugly, small and petite, she'd never really exuded radiance, intelligence, or anything impressive, not even in her teens. It was her youngest sister that had indeed fitted the bill there, in all its entirety. Taller than her siblings, a photographic memory and intellectual, pretty too; Melinda had remained in the background whilst the siblings were all young and living at home. Just a number, she was, the eldest of a litter of five, that was how she had portrayed herself.

As regards relationships though, Melinda had been a sibling that was dedicated to her marriage and her children, then later on, her grandchildren (not insinuating that the others weren't). Work-wise, Melinda had always been employed, even with the children small. Part-time jobs bringing in a small pay packet to help with the utility bills, allowing her to spend some precious time with the family. Normality and security, two important words in Melinda's vocabulary; with all said and done though, she was still just a number. One that had kept going throughout the rough times in her life, coming out the other side no worse for wear, but wiser for it, a lot wiser.

Careful and thrifty, the holidays that had occurred with Peter's and Melinda's hard earned funds, wonderful places that had elapsed over the years, but remembered for the wide experiences of everything discovered. From a caravan break in Fishguard, to an Alaskan cruise; revelling at the glaciers in front of their eyes and watching the dolphins heading towards the cruise liner, in pairs. Hawaii had been registered for its beauty, sunshine, and Elvis Presley, of course; Las Vegas also depicting Peter's love for the idol that he had never seen in real life, but visiting the places he had sung his heart out in before his death at such an early age.

In reality, Melinda's life thus far wasn't nearly as bad as other people she had connected with; she was happy with her lot. Learning to live with herself as a person, had given her plenty of delight, struggles, and indeed hard times throughout her years. There was more to come, much more. Amanda would see to that, for sure. From bingo buddies to holiday companions, along with a friendship that had lasted years; she counted herself as lucky, very lucky.

Melinda's years with Peter as a couple was a memory to treasure. He'd drawn the short straw in not being able to indulge in more memories from around the globe, whilst being free from working and in retirement age. It hadn't happened, but life is never straightforward, and sadly no-one can complete everything written down on their bucket list, well almost no-one. The ones that do are in the minority, for sure.

Melinda's holiday of a lifetime, Alaska and the Canadian Rockies, had gone ahead even though she wasn't sure her cancer would get her first. Peter's dream break to America; Memphis, Tupelo, and Graceland, Elvis Presley's home, to name just a few areas travelled, was Melinda's husband's guilty pleasure. A holiday booked secretly, giving him a whopping surprise to treasure, and indeed it was. Peter had loved every minute of it.

The future is so uncertain, as is life, but with the best will in the world, disappointments are a necessary action. Holding the key to happiness is something that has to be worked at, each and every day. Confidence grows through trial and error, and unfortunately doesn't come handed on a plate. Melinda's aunty, a favourite of hers, had insinuated that she had ants in her pants; as a child she couldn't sit still. Nothing had changed there, more than fifty years on.

Holidays since Fuerteventura has been halted by the coronavirus epidemic, now apparent in most countries of the globe. A pandemic that has caused misery and untold deaths, through no fault of their own. Patience is a virtue, so, so true. With communication now mainly by telephone, the hopes and fears are forever prominent now, just trying to stay safe being all too important. If, and when the evil virus disappears, then maybe life can resume again for Melinda, and everyone on earth that are so dear to her.

Walking to Amanda's business address, Melinda had resumed her somewhat boring day to day existence, and had her friend pencil in a date for more foot treatment when her shop was able to re-open. Amanda had busied herself with cleaning everything around in preparation for that day to come. Fuerteventura had taught Melinda a lesson. If you don't try, then you won't know if you can succeed. Melinda was determined to succeed!

Epilogue

Melinda's childhood had been much like any others in the neighbourhood. Luxuries were non-existent, but weren't missed either. Knowing no difference to other children around, days were enjoyed regardless. With large families all around, there was always children of a similar age to play with and keep each other company, brothers and sisters of known children in their classroom.

Being the eldest of five siblings, Melinda had a friend in her class, who was one of six siblings. Melinda's brothers and sisters, she had two of each, were also friends with her brothers and sisters. The local park, only minutes away from their houses, was where they had played after school. Just two families, but altogether there were eleven children engrossed in play, until Melinda's mum and Jean's mum had called them all in when food was on the table.

New clothes were a rare purchase and Melinda had felt a little sorry for her youngest sister, who, after items became too small for Melinda, had been handed down to Melanie, and then down to her. Twice a year Amelia had taken them shopping for an outfit, to wear on Easter Sunday and on Christmas Day. They had all felt so special, then. Buying second-hand clothes from charity shops and jumble sales, everyone around them were doing exactly the same, so they hadn't felt left out, no different at all.

Melinda's parents had given them all chores to do and although facial jibs were shown when told what they had to do, they had done whatever was asked of them, eventually; though sometimes putting up a fight, rhetorically speaking, beforehand. Melinda could still hear her siblings murmuring under their breath, 'Do I have to?'

As the years had passed, earning a small wager for cooking the tea every evening, running a paper-round to save up for fashions of the era, popular clothing of that time, Melinda had learnt a lot of life's lessons. It hadn't done her any harm, not really. She was well prepared for marriage and having her children, by the time she had turned eighteen. Admittedly, Melinda had always been the quiet and serious child, compared to her siblings, but that wasn't always a bad thing. Being a bit of a loner, she had enjoyed dressmaking and relaxed completely when following her hobby. Her aunty Peggy had learnt her to knit, along with her mother, creating jumpers and cardigans from difficult patterns. She'd even knitted a woollen bikini with the help of her aunty Peggy once, bright orange in colour. What was she thinking back then?

Peter, being the baby of five siblings, had been spoilt, if that was possible back then. With a thirteen year age gap between his eldest sister and him, he had gotten away with a lot more than the others. Peter's dad was, similar to Melinda's dad, quite disciplined. Different scenarios, but both equally ruling the roost. He would never argue with his dad, but had on one occasion caused the police to knock on the door, disrespecting his father, with him receiving the brunt of

Peter's actions. Only a young child, he had felt so remorseful, and when years later, his son had done the same thing to him, the tables turned had signalled in his mind; realising the hurt his dad had felt, and the similar hurt Peter was receiving, then. Sadly, Peter had never received an apology from his son, whether warranted or not (Peter could be stubborn at times). His actions as a child had haunted him, something he could never forget, and Thomas's actions had brought it all to the surface, sadly. Peter had passed away without seeing his eldest son, his first born child. Thomas was holidaying in Lanzarote with his family at the time.

Melinda and Peter were in sync with each other, most of the time. Both working to bring in the best salaries they could and give their son and daughter the best lives possible. Things weren't always perfect, no marriage ever was. Disagreements over the years were far and few between.

With Peter the manual worker who was hands on with a screwdriver and a paintbrush, amongst other implements in the do-it-yourself range, Melinda was adept at paperwork, basically keeping control of the bills and financial situation.

More at home when dealing with office work and the like, her last job on the employment rung of the ladder was as a deputy manager in a well-known bookmakers. Head work was Melinda's forte, along with dealing with customers, clients etc. A people person they both were, though stressful at times. Their vocations were ideal for their individual characters, Peter being the clown amongst them. Both were sticklers for perfection, as regards each individual jobs.

Peter had been dumbstruck when Melinda was diagnosed with breast cancer, with Stephanie absolutely gobsmacked when told. She had always worried about her dad's health, but had never considered her mum becoming ill. Melinda was always there to iron out the creases, put everything into order, and look after the family, with no exceptions. Stephanie's mum's illness had upset the apple cart, everything the family had represented. Shock was a word that was usually taken for granted, unknown to either of them before then.

When Melinda was given the "all clear" five years later, followed by Peter's lung cancer diagnosis that was terminal, feathers were well and truly ruffled. Stephanie was absolutely beside herself, even with her career in the medical profession. Peter was her dad, a man she had idolised; Melinda always knew that she was a daddy's girl.

Life was lived as best they could, considering. From being nursed through her breast cancer, Melinda was now nursing her husband, with a diagnosis that would eventually be fatal. There were no words on Peter's death; a lot of thinking and reminiscing, with a lot of upset and tears. A conclusion that hadn't been wanted, but was inevitable, in the end.

Sixty-six years of age wasn't old and Peter hadn't felt his age, even at the end of his illness. With his continuing wit and hopefulness, he had laughed through his condition when able to, but his need to digest and fulfil his appetite with a final meal of a well-done steak and chips, something that hadn't happened due to having to be fed through his stomach as time had progressed, had Melinda feeling bitterly disappointed. Even now, she feels guilty when eating the meal that Peter had so craved for. Would he be eating it where he was now? Melinda had so hoped he was.

A poem found on the social media, had Melinda in tears, but knowing the words would represent her husband's beliefs so accurately, it was something Melinda had wanted to share in A Time to Remember.

I'm Still Here

I may be gone but please don't cry
Death is not the last goodbyes
Death releases me of my pain
There will come a day we will meet again
Don't be blue and don't be sad
Think back to the fun we had
I am always here I hear you speak
In time of trouble, it's me you seek
You don't see me but I see you
I will do my best to pull you through
Speak to me and I will hear
Never far I am always near
Be brave my love do not cry
See you again, it's not goodbye.

John F Connor